*For Sylvia,
may you
enjoy reading
as much as
writing it.
Ian*

IAN RUNCIE

Ian Runcie is a Doctor. He lives in Sussex, with his wife and two daughters.

Front cover design by author. Photograph from Werner Forman Archive, London: rock carvings at Vitlycke Museum, Bohuslän, Sweden.

© Copyright 2005 Ian Runcie.

All rights reserved. No part of this publication may be reproduced, stored in a retrieval system, or transmitted, in any form or by any means, electronic, mechanical, photocopying, recording, or otherwise, without the written prior permission of the author.

Note for Librarians: a cataloguing record for this book that includes Dewey Decimal Classification and US Library of Congress numbers is available from the Library and Archives of Canada. The complete cataloguing record can be obtained from their online database at: www.collectionscanada.ca/amicus/index-e.html
ISBN 1-4120-2628-8

Printed in Victoria, BC, Canada

Printed on paper with minimum 30% recycled fibre. Trafford's print shop runs on "green energy" from solar, wind and other environmentally-friendly power sources.

TRAFFORD *Offices in Canada, USA, Ireland and UK*

This book was published *on-demand* in cooperation with Trafford Publishing. On-demand publishing is a unique process and service of making a book available for retail sale to the public taking advantage of on-demand manufacturing and Internet marketing. On-demand publishing includes promotions, retail sales, manufacturing, order fulfilment, accounting and collecting royalties on behalf of the author.

Book sales for North America and international:
Trafford Publishing, 6E–2333 Government St.,
Victoria, BC v8t 4p4 CANADA
phone 250 383 6864 (toll-free 1 888 232 4444)
fax 250 383 6804; email to orders@trafford.com

Book sales in Europe:
Trafford Publishing (uk) Ltd., Enterprise House, Wistaston Road Business Centre,
Wistaston Road, Crewe, Cheshire cw2 7rp UNITED KINGDOM
phone 01270 251 396 (local rate 0845 230 9601)
facsimile 01270 254 983; orders.uk@trafford.com

Order online at:
trafford.com/05-0456

10   9   8   7

IAN RUNCIE

ALBERICH AND FRIENDS

To Hannah: may the birds fly back soon.

Thanks

To my family for their encouragement. Also to Jan Bowman, Vanessa Brown and Hazel Phelan for their proof-reading skills and many helpful suggestions.

Contents

Chapters

1	Alberich	9
2	Fricka	15
3	Loge	25
4	Donner	32
5	The Volsungs	41
6	Brünnhilde 1	59
7	Brünnhilde 2	67
8	Mime	72
9	Fafner	81
10	Siegfried	87
11	The Gibichungs	97

Epilogue: Wotan — 121

Appendices

1	Sources	125
2	The Ring Cycle	127
3	Philosophy	130

Notes — 135

Bibliography — 149

Links — 150

Acknowledgements and Explanations

Many interpretations of Wagner's Ring contributed to the sentiments in this book. I am particularly indebted to Robert Donnington for his psychological study without which none of the following chapters could have been written. Also to Bryan Magee for his study of Wagner's philosophical progress.

Those who are looking for an explanation of the story of the Ring should be wary of this book for it does not follow Wagner's story exactly. The extensive notes are designed to fill the gaps. A change in font denotes 'thoughts' or stream of conciousness of the character in question.

A number of different translations of the libretti have been utilised. By far the most quoted is from www.rwagner.net/ but, apart from Brünnhilde's speech in the notes, very little is a straight translation and the text has been adapted for the novel format.

For anyone unfamiliar with the nature of mythology it may be helpful to know that climacteric events may not mean quite the same to the inhabitants of the mythological worlds as they do to us. Death may stand for transformation. A murderer may find himself taking on some of the characteristics of the dead individual. Keeping it in the family by incestuous methods is often the preferred method of procreation amongst Gods, although the more conservative of the Gods may not approve of such activity, especially where mortals are concerned. This is helped along by the knowledge that divine reproduction may not follow the same physiological principles with which we are familiar. With regard to the allegorical nature of mythology and magic: too much explanation can get in the way of understanding and that gets me, rather neatly, off a very big hook.

As this book is based on the Ring cycle, I could perhaps have legitimately used the future tense throughout but this makes for tedious reading (and writing). I have however moved freely between the present and past tenses with some deliberate intent. For the most part, the present tense is utilised to move the action along. We are sitting in the opera house with the action skipping along at Wagnerian speed. In the past tense we are sitting in our favourite chair, reading and contemplating.

"The Ring stands there like a multi-faceted mirror. When you look at it you see fragments of yourself."

Adapted from Keith Warner.

Chapter 1. Alberich

IN the days before anyone could come along and build a castle, the beauty and mystery of the Rhine were unsurpassed.

The river rises near the mountain home of the Gods, crashes into the valleys of Middle Earth and oozes its way through the swampy plains to enter the sea through a deep channel at the far western edge of Europe. We may be within the warm, deep, barely flowing water or gliding wraith-like through the thickness of the steam rising from its surface. Or perhaps we are standing on the swampy shore, vaguely aware of the towering mountains glimpsed at intervals through the thick wandering mist. The rocks are jagged and haphazard and the land is tilted, suggesting a recent massive geological upheaval. The only sound is the drone of the slow water, which is increasing gradually as we become conscious of movement in the mud of the river floor. We catch a glimpse of a quick-tailed amphibious creature emerging from the mud, heading for the bank and becoming lost in the swirling mud and mist.

As the mist clears again, it seems that we may have been mistaken, for the lone figure we can now see stumbling out of the water and along the rocks and swamps clearly has two legs. There is nothing beautiful about the appearance or the thoughts of this creature for following him there is a swell on the surface of the water which, to those of us who understand these things, predicts change, violence and disorder.

Dwarfs were probably fairly common at that time but most were satisfied with living underground, digging for their precious metals and fashioning fine weapons and jewellery. Alberich had always known he was different. Even though the light hurt his eyes he, seemingly alone of dwarfs, was aware of the beauty and the mystery of the Rhine. As usual his thoughts were turning to the tales of Wotan. There was a legend that the blood of Wotan flowed in Alberich's ancestry. Was Wotan really all-powerful? Wotan was said to live in eternal light, to be tall, graceful and eloquent, to have wisdom and power: everything, in fact, that Alberich lacked. Alberich's concern was not that he lacked powerful magic, for he had spent many hours perfecting his understanding while his less aware companions were delving deeper into the mines of Nibelung. As a youth, he had isolated himself from his contemporaries by giving free expression to what they saw as wild ravings and dangerous ideas. He had tried and failed to interest his fellow dwarfs in achieving more than just the products of their work. His companions had responded by trying to tease, cajole and threaten him into conforming but after feeling the lash of his tongue and experiencing his increasing strength and power, one by one they had left him alone. Eventually Alberich had welcomed this for he concluded that his fellow dwarfs were incapable of advancement. Frustrated by the world as he found it, he felt powerless and ignored with no outlet for his abilities. For many years he remained isolated and dissatisfied, raging against the established order. Approaching maturity he embraced a radical and violent philosophy that required nothing less than the wholesale destruction of the society around him. He felt that those in power, whom he never managed to identify with certainty, were determined to retain their elevated status and maintain a system that ensured that no member of the race of dwarfs could ever gain a position of influence. The inertia of his fellow dwarfs was unhelpful to his cause but this he considered to be the result of years of neglect and subtle propaganda that ensured that dwarfs were incapable of improvement. Alberich reached the conclusion that it was necessary for oppressed races to rise up, take control and build a society in which all had their allocated proper work and position and all would receive fulfilment in accordance with their needs. Nothing less than a conflagration of the works of men and the Gods was necessary to achieve these aims.[1] After this event, love, mutual respect and equality between the races are all that would be required.

But love had eluded Alberich.

As he grew older he had come to realise with great bitterness that his perfect society would never come about, just as his own quest for love would never be satisfied. His ambitions became warped, more personal and many thought evil. Why should a dwarf with his abilities be denied a position of power? He began to consider himself as a valid alternative to Wotan and was convinced that he would be able to manage the world in a rather more ordered and efficient manner. His bitterness warped even his appreciation of nature. To see the Rhine covered in dwarfish industrial enterprise, factories and smoke, all of them working for his own advancement was more in keeping with his desires. He regretted that there were still things he did not understand enough to challenge the world successfully. Take that swell in the river as he walked along. It seemed to be following him and Alberich did not doubt that it was related to his own thoughts. But it was not his magic and not under his control. Under whose control was it? Wotan's? Something deeper than Wotan?

Suddenly he became stock-still and stared at the river: his only movement a slow waggle of his beard. Two Rhinemaidens[2] were cavorting in the water, riding the swell and singing. Their naked shoulders flashed out of the water, their hair floated behind them, almost the same length as their bodies. He saw they were laughing at a third companion who was scolding them, apparently for not doing their work properly.

Alberich was helplessly drawn by their magic lure. Totally seduced, he forgot his rather repulsive appearance and offered, almost joyously, to join them cavorting in the river. At first the Rhinemaidens were frightened but once they saw Alberich they were amused. One by one each of them encouraged him with lewd suggestions and gestures but, as soon as he began to scramble over the rocks and through the river towards them, they laughed and swam out of his reach making cruel jokes about his appearance, calling him names like "hairy humpbacked horror" and "swarthy, scaly, sulphurous dwarf". Alberich finally realised that, once again, he was being teased and he was not going to seduce one of these creatures. Why should these desirable fish with human skin be allowed to make fun of him? He was furious. Suddenly he realised that his fury was the key required to disturb the Gods. Finally he would show the world that he was not a figure of fun. With spider-like agility he ran over the rocks and through the water, grabbing at the Rhinemaidens and occasionally almost catching them. Madly he roared:

> "Through all my frame what passionate fires rage
> and longings burn and glow, turning me to madness.
> Though you may laugh and lie, lustfully I long for
> you and one of you shall yield to me."

Perhaps in response to his fury, the sun's rays rose over the hills, dispersing the mists and lighting up a glittering warm reflection in the water. Immediately the impetuous Rhinemaidens forgot Alberich and with the sun's rays reflecting on their tails they began leaping in the water like dolphins and singing,

> "Rhinegold, Rhinegold.
> What radiant joy.
> Your glistening beams dance over the waves
> What games we shall play."

"What is it my glossy ones?"   Cried Alberich

The Rhinemaidens laughed, surprised that Alberich did not know about the gold. In their excitement two of them told Alberich its secret.
> "Only he who renounces love may have the gold and only he who gains the magic to forge a ring from the gold may rule the world.
> Therefore we are secure and free from care, for all that live will love, and no-one from love's fetters would be free: least of all love sick gnomes!
> Come, enjoy the gold, bask in its radiance and laugh with us."

The swell on the water rose several metres. The third Rhine-maiden was horrified and warned the others, "Remember Father warned us to guard the gold against those who would steal it."

But she was too late.

To renounce love is a terrible act but for Alberich love was rare indeed. Had he not just offered love to the Rhinemaidens, only to be rebuffed once again? If he could not have love, could he not obtain pleasure by might? This, he knows, is his chance. He hesitates only briefly before using his immense dwarfish strength to dive against the rising swell of the river to the gold. His lust for the Rhinemaidens is forgotten in his seething desire for gold and power. No longer interested in their swirling bodies he brushes aside the screaming mermaids, telling them to flirt in the dark in future. Rapaciously he tears the gold from its resting place, gathering up huge handfuls to drag down through the mud to where the Rhinemaidens cannot follow. Repeatedly he shouts foul blasphemies: cursing and forswearing love.

> "My hand quenches your light, as I wrest your gold from the rock.
> And I will fashion the ring of revenge.
> Hear me, you waves, may love be accursed for ever!"

Chapter 2: Fricka

IT is said that Wotan lost an eye[3] to gain wisdom but the wisdom of the Gods moves in mysterious ways: ways which do not always impress their wives.

To mortal eyes, Asgard, the mist-walled and cloud-carpeted mountain peaks of the Gods appear indistinct and fragile but to Fricka[4] and the other Gods they are substantial enough. At dawn on the day of payment Fricka woke early to find Wotan still sleeping. They were lying together on one of the flower-covered peaks, well above the clouds and warm in the early morning sun. Fricka prodded Wotan awake and was immediately sorry for as he opened his eye, still half dreaming, he started to talk of the fame his newly completed castle would bring. As he woke further and the pleasant dream of longing left him, mist started to swirl and howl around the tops in response to his mood. Fricka could see that Wotan was now well aware of the problems this day would bring. Wotan groaned, adjusted his eye patch and picked up his spear. Fricka too groaned; this spear had always irritated her. It represented both the source and the vulnerability of Wotan's power. It catalogued both his wisdom and his folly, for on it were carved his contracts and his deals. Wotan had fashioned the spear from a branch of the world ash tree and, sometime later, had managed to hang himself from the same tree for nine days, after piercing himself in the side with the spear. Apparently he had done this as part of his quest to gain wisdom. Fricka could never understand why Wotan had to make so many contracts and to repeatedly wander away from the security of his home and family. Recently he appeared even more remote than usual and was refusing to discuss anything of importance with her. He appeared to be obsessed by the need to impress his subjects and to protect himself from his enemies. These enemies seemed to Fricka to be mostly the results of his own imagination. Wotan was a God who knew his own frailties and he also knew that, but for these frailties, he could reign supreme. No sooner had he made laws and commandments than there were exceptions to be considered, doubts to be explored and personal passions to be accommodated. Wotan's spear was therefore heavily scored. Fricka considered it necessary to deal with her followers by imposing rigid rules of conduct: creating systems that promised apparent immortality for loyalty and eternal discomfort for those who dared to question her word. This, she knew, is the only way religious leaders are able to achieve the necessary power over their subjects and create the circumstances whereby their followers would be prepared to sacrifice themselves for his or her cause. There is, of course, an unfortunate necessity for the leaders to apparently abide by their own laws and behave in the manner they themselves prescribe. Otherwise they would be in peril when their subjects realised that their leaders' position and creations may not be as substantial as they had been led to believe. Fricka was happy with this requirement but it was not a major feature of Wotan's creed. Recently, Fricka had been particularly worried because, in his blacker moods and despite his recent building work, Wotan appeared to have developed a desire to destroy so many of the things he had previously achieved. She also sensed that Wotan had another mysterious concern, so grave that he was not yet able to voice it.

Fricka was the Goddess of marriage and law; convention and precedence were her remit. As such, she knew that it was she, herself, who held the ultimate power. Why else had Wotan wooed her? She had no time for Wotan's inconsistencies and talk of seeking wisdom. She was sure that, if he were only to abandon change and exploration, most of his problems would be solved. Through the mist Fricka could glimpse the castle. It was massive, with an impressively solid appearance but apparently floating in the clouds, as if it had no foundations. This was her husband's new Valhalla[5]: built by two giants as an impregnable fortress against his enemies. The prospect of living there had originally filled Fricka with excitement for she had hopes of a more settled and homely existence. Her excitement had soon been replaced by anxiety when she had heard of the payment arrangements, for they seemed to threaten the very existence of the Gods. Wotan had agreed to allow the giants to take possession of Fricka's sister and favourite companion, Freya. Freya[6] was the Goddess of youth and supplied the golden apples that were the Gods' source of eternal youth and life. Whenever Freya was near there was brightness in the air and a feeling of contentment that was important to Fricka. Freya had an easy charm and was liked by almost everyone she met. She had an ability to put people at their ease and, even following the briefest of conversations, would leave one feeling she had a particular interest in them alone. She was a great prize and possessed qualities that the Gods were otherwise lacking. Fricka knew that Wotan had no intention of making this payment. She also knew that, as chief of the Gods, he had to honour his contracts and he now needed to persuade the giants to accept some other payment. Wotan had kept her well away from the negotiations with the giants and now she knew why. She would never have allowed him to make such a disgraceful arrangement in his thirst for control. She despaired at the decietful lengths men would go to in their quest for power over others. When she had complained to Wotan, he had merely mentioned how she herself had begged him for the new castle. She had responded by saying that her reasons for wanting the castle were for the family and to help persuade her errant husband from wandering away from her. All she had wanted was a fine home but he had built a fortress, which could only result in more unrest. Wotan had replied that, as a supreme God, possession of a palace that his subjects could admire was essential to persuade the outside world to continue to support him. Was it not Fricka who believed that all Gods needed to impress and subdue their followers, and what better way to do this than to create mighty buildings? He had also remarked that those who loved life as much as he did also loved roaming and variety. When Fricka accused him of being unloving towards her, Wotan had reminded her that he had lost his eye in order to gain her. Fricka suspected him of lying.

As usual in such matters, the arrangement for paying the giants was the idea of Loge who had promised Wotan that some substitute payment would be found. Fricka disliked Loge intensely and assumed that the other Gods felt the same. Loge was the God of fire and patron of smiths. Constantly in motion, which his slight lameness only served to make more annoying, he had an irritating way of dissolving into fire at inopportune moments. He also had a way of discovering one's weaknesses and of mentioning them at times when Fricka wished he wouldn't. She felt Wotan should not allow Loge to get away with some of his comments to her. Worst of all, Loge was a frequent companion of Wotan on his silly excursions to Middle-Earth and sometimes even the underworld. There they would consort freely with the likes of giants, dwarfs and men. Fricka was never quite sure whether these adventures were Loge's ideas or Wotan's. She glared at her husband, for now that the castle was finished, there was of course no sign of the God of fire.

Fricka was startled out of her contemplation by the arrival of Freya who ran to her and threw herself at her feet, grabbing her dress. No brightness or contentment was apparent now for Freya was closely followed by the two giants, Fafner and Fasolt, swinging their huge clubs and demanding that she came back with them to their lair. Fricka was offended that these uncouth creatures should be allowed anywhere near her home and, as for taking away Freya, the idea was laughable. How could they imagine that Wotan had meant to keep such a bargain? There had been a time when, purely by virtue of their size and physical strength, the giants had ruled much of the Middle-Earth. Wotan had managed to tame most of them by playing on their slow wits with the usual combination of threats of Donner's hammer and hell-fire, versus promises of eternal bliss. Middle-Earth was undoubtedly more peaceful as a result but the tameness of the giants remained precarious.

Freya's shouting and the noise of the giants attracted Freya's brothers, Froh and Donner.[7] Fricka was concerned about the look on Donner's face. Although he was the God of war, he was rather sweet. He was, however, very jealous where Freya was concerned and far too fond of her for Fricka's conventional ideas. He was already becoming very red in the face and swinging his hammer about in a way that suggested a lot of unnecessary bad weather. As for Froh, he may be able to make rainbows, but nobody is really sure what he is for; perhaps we shall find out. Wotan sighed loudly and, finding no sign of Loge, tried to laugh the matter off by telling the giants that the offer of Freya was obviously a joke and they should name another price. The giants were surprised to learn that the Gods were capable of duplicity and were not going to be put off so easily, for Fafner wanted the apples and eternal youth and Fasolt had obviously fallen hopelessly in love with Freya. In their slow and pedantic fashion they pointed out that a price had been agreed and they had delivered the castle just as Wotan required. Fasolt, quite reasonably, reminded Wotan that he was unable to break a contract without undermining his own position and causing a revolt against his own power.

> "You have more wisdom than we have wits.
> You have bound us giants to keep the peace, when previously we were free.
> I will curse all your wisdom and flee from your peace if you do not keep faith in your bond.
> A simple giant counsels you thus."

He went on to declare his love for Freya demonstrating a surprising degree of insight in the process.

> "You radiant race, who rule by beauty, how foolishly you strive for towers of stone
> and pledge a woman's beauty for fortress and hall.
> We dullards toil away with our horny hands.
> Sweating, to win a woman who is winsome and gentle and will live with us.
> Now you try to deny us!"

FRICKA

Fafner called him a fool and made it clear that his main aim was to deprive the Gods of their power by removing their golden apples. He grabbed at Freya intending to remove her by force. All this made the other Gods furious. Donner raised his hammer to deal violently with the giants, forcing Wotan to stop him with his spear. Wotan knew Fasolt was correct and that, however corrupt the deals, politics and negotiations recorded on the spear may be, they are always preferable to the power of violence and the hammer.

At this moment of impasse, there is a shimmer in the air and Loge suddenly appears in a flash of flame. Wotan is clearly relieved but Fricka groans, "Why does he have to be such a trickster?" Loge states that he has searched the whole world but has been unable to find a price that men will accept in exchange for a woman's worth.

Fricka sees her chance and wails, "See Wotan what a traitorous knave you have trusted."

Donner too is unable to control himself, "Accursed flame I will quench your glow." He roars, much to Loge's amusement.

Freya cries to her brothers to help her for it seems that Wotan is about to betray her.

Wotan supports his companion. "Wait all of you. You do not know my friend nor his craft. His counsel is always the better the slower it is given. When courage alone is required I do not ask for help but when craft and cunning are necessary, Loge is the master. Wait no longer Loge. Keep your word."

But Fricka knows that Loge will take his time and fumes inwardly while he spins out his story. First he points out the ingratitude of the other Gods for, while they were sleeping, he has tested the fortress and has found it strong and well built. The giants' work is reliable, they clearly deserve their pay and their arguments are quite correct. He reminds them all how Wotan wanted a fortress and Fricka a stately home and how Donner and Froh would need a house and court should they marry. Slowly he tells of his travels and how he has learned from the Rhinemaidens that the Nibelung dwarf, Alberich has forsworn love, stolen the Rhinemaiden's gold and has forged a ring from the gold, which has enabled him to enslave the other dwarfs. Already he was adding to his massive hoard of riches and enslaved followers. In return for this information, Loge says that he had promised to ask Wotan to ensure that the gold is returned to the Rhinemaidens. Wotan roars that he is already in enough trouble but, as Loge expected, the giants are also showing interest. The giants muse that they have had previous dealings with Alberich and with these riches and, in particular, the ring, he might become very troublesome indeed.

Loge then carries on to tell them all of the ring and its legendary power over the entire world. The Gods are concerned, for this implies a much greater threat to their own position than these simple giants. Wotan is less concerned than the others and gloats to himself.

"I have heard talk of the Rhine's gold.
This ring would give unbounded power and wealth."

Fricka grudgingly admires Loge's abilities and asks if the gold could be turned into glittering gems such as a woman of her status might admire. Insultingly, Loge replies,

FRICKA

"A wife could ensure her husband's fidelity if she decked herself with such bright ornament."

Fricka gasps and turns to Wotan but all he says is,

"I must have the ring."

Wotan asks Loge if it would be necessary to forswear love to obtain it.
"That you must not do." Says Loge but suggests that the ring might be obtained by theft from Alberich who, after all, was no more than a thief himself. Then the gold should be returned to the Rhinemaidens as he had promised.

Wotan refuses,
"The Rhinemaidens?
What is this counsel to me?"

Fricka agrees
"I wish to know nothing of that watery brood.
Many a man - to my sorrow -
have they lured with their seductive sport."

The giants also remain interested. Fafner turns to Fasolt,
"Believe me, that glittering gold is worth more than Freya.
For eternal youth he gains who commands the gold's magic"

He then turns to Wotan.
"Hear, Wotan, what we have to say.
Freya may stay with you in peace.
An easier fee I've found in settlement.
We rough giants would be satisfied with the Nibelung's shining gold."

Wotan is cornered and feels the results of his own duplicity closing in on him.
"Have you lost your senses?
Can I give you what I do not own?
Shall I exert myself against the gnome for you?
You fools!
My debt to you has made you shameless and over-covetous.

Suddenly the giants gather up Freya and march away, announcing that they are taking Freya as hostage until evening. Despite Freya's screams, the Gods seem unable to stop them as the source of their eternal youth is carried off. Only Loge, who is not reliant on the apples, appears to be unaffected. Wotan's beard seems greyer, Donner drops his hammer and Froh loses his colour. The region darkens and Fricka feels old.

Chapter 3: Loge

Loge was a cynic and not always wise.

Fiendishly intelligent and intuitively aware of human and celestial folly: he was as contemptuous of his fellow men and Gods, as he was desirous of their company and admiration. Bored with repetitive behaviour and dullness, he would flit from one situation to the next and from one person to the next. The more unpopular he became the more he felt the need to goad his companions. Even when he was being helpful, Loge could not resist his own destructive streak. He was particularly prone to annoying Fricka for, in truth, he was jealous of her relationship with Wotan. Fricka stood for all that Loge felt deprived of and all he felt a need to destroy: family, safety, contentment, and complacency. Would his mind never rest? Only occasionally when he was alone with Wotan was he able to stem his own restlessness and reach contentment, but even Wotan seemed misguided and preoccupied these days.

Loge[8] outlined a plan to obtain the gold, which depended on his assessment of Alberich's inflated pride in his own achievements. He and Wotan became excited and wasted no time in descending to the underworld to seek out Alberich. Loge slyly suggested a route to the mines of Nibelheim via the Rhine but Wotan immediately refused, knowing full well that Loge's purpose was to meet the Rhinemaidens on the way. Instead they took a route via a sulphurous cleft in the rocks above the mines. This acted as a vent for the fires of the dwarfs and through it they were able to reach the mines undetected. They entered a vast noisy underground cavern, lit by flaming torches and furnace fires. The cavern was full of dwarfs, all working to Alberich's orders, hammering unceasingly on anvils and piling up gold. As the two Gods crept in, they recognised Alberich's brother, Mime, whom they knew to be a smith of great skill. Mime was running around, howling and throwing up his arms to protect himself, as if being set upon by an invisible assailant. When this had stopped, and Mime was recovering, the Gods stealthily approached him and discovered that Alberich had just forced Mime to forge a magic chain–mail helmet from the rhinegold. Given the name 'Tarnhelm' by Alberich, the helmet allowed whoever wore it to take on any form they wished. Mime had forged Tarnhelm to Alberich's specifications and then, in order to escape, had tried to work out its magic function. Alberich had caught him and had demonstrated its function by putting it on, becoming invisible, and beating him. Loge was concerned that he and Wotan had not been able to see Alberich, even in a shadowy form. This was dangerous. He hoped that Alberich would not yet feel powerful enough to try out the ring on the Gods.

Mime told them that the ring somehow ensured that the dwarfs obeyed Alberich's will and whip. Alberich was forcing the Nibelungs to work almost without rest. No longer were they carefree smiths, enjoying their craft, but were slaves to Alberich's semi-mechanical methods for producing ever-increasing amounts of gold. Wotan was

LOGE

amused by an unusual degree of concern on the part of Loge for Mime and noticed a considerable physical resemblance between the two. He wondered if perhaps Alberich and Mime might be only half brothers[9]. He easily resisted the temptation to chide Loge, as he knew he would have to answer for his own rumoured role in the ancestry of the remarkable but troublesome pair.

Alberich has taken off Tarnhelm and appears in another part of the cave where the two Gods make themselves known to him. He greets them with mocking politeness, asking why they have come. Loge sets about flattering him, saying that Alberich's wealth and cleverness were famous, even in Asgard, and they had come to see for themselves. To goad Alberich he points out that only by the power of his fire could Alberich fashion his gold. Alberich responds by declaring that he no longer fears nor does he need the Gods' powers.

> " The hoard shall be worked by the Nibelung and by its power will I rule the world.
> This gold shall enslave you. Your men shall bow to my might and your women who spurn my wooing shall yield to my force. Love no longer smiles on me so beware for, just as I have forsworn love, all who have life shall also forswear it."

"Blasphemous fool!" Shouts Wotan.

But Loge is worried and whispers to Wotan to keep his head. To Alberich he allows himself to appear impressed.
> "Even the moon, the stars and the sun shall be your slaves. Now what if a thief crept up slyly and stole your gold while you were asleep?"

Alberich tells him that he is not the fool Loge thinks, and could protect himself with Tarnhelm, which allows him to take any form he wants. Loge feigns disbelief and accuses him of lying. Alberich laughs and, in front of the Gods, turns himself rapidly into a huge snake. Loge appears suitably frightened. He is frightened - not by the snake - but by the power of Tarnhelm and ultimately the ring. Loge considers that some weakening of the power of the Gods might not be regretted, but the world under the sway of this evil could not be tolerated. Alberich with overall political power was a situation he feared for he could see that Alberich would not stop at the control of the dwarfs. Alberich would soon need help and would naturally turn to man for assistance. Alberich in control of the minds of men was, to Loge, a prospect of doom, for men could be relentless in their evil. With only slight encouragement, they would gladly organise themselves into an armed and uniformed group in support of Alberich. There was only one sound in Middle Earth that Loge really feared- the sound of marching men.

After a nudge from Loge, Wotan forces himself to join in and expresses great admiration for Alberich's abilities.

"A large serpent is all very well." Says Loge, but could Alberich turn himself into something small that could hide easily when required: a toad for instance? As Alberich obliges, Loge and Wotan are ready. Chasing the half formed toad around the cave, Wotan eventually manages to stand on it and Loge swiftly removes the Tarnhelm. It is all a little too easy. As Alberich becomes a Dwarf again, they bind him and carry him off to Asgard. Here they taunt him about his plans for taking over the world and force him to pay a ransom in return for his freedom. Furious but impotent, he kisses the ring thus communicating with his slaves and ordering them to bring the gold to Asgard.

LOGE

Although ashamed to be seen in this situation, he does not appear too concerned and mutters to himself.

> "What a fool I have been. To get myself free I must pay the ransom.
> But terrible revenge shall follow.
> If I keep only the ring, I could easily spare the treasure.
> For new wealth would soon be won at the ring's command.
> This is a warning to make me wise.
> I shall not pay too dear for my education if the lesson costs me only these baubles."

As the slaves pile up the gold around him, Wotan demands to keep the Tarnhelm. Alberich is now distressed but, again, considers quietly:

> "Accursed thief, Wotan, but he who made the helmet may be made to make another."

But just as Alberich thinks he had paid all, Wotan demands the ring on his finger.
Now Alberich is distraught, he accuses Wotan of being a thief and threatens that the theft of the ring will bring terrible consequences. Even Alberich is shocked that the guardian of morality and law can compromise himself in this way. Alberich says that he would rather lose his life than the ring but Wotan calmly replies that the ring is all that is necessary and Alberich may do what he likes with his life.
Alberich cries,

> "Take heed, haughty God!
> If I sinned, I sinned only against myself.
> But you, immortal one, sin against all that was, all that is and all that shall be: if you seize my ring!"

Unworried, Wotan forcibly tears the ring from Alberich's finger pointing out that Alberich is no more than a thief himself.

> "Defeated, destroyed!" wails Alberich, as Wotan shouts triumphantly:

> "This ring lifts me on high and I shall be the mightiest lord of all."

Loge does not like Wotan's violent acts and triumphal shouts. He feels the ring has been obtained by dubious means and would clearly be best left with the Rhinemaidens, as he had promised. He is even beginning to be concerned that the ring, in Wotan's hands, may be worse than in Alberich's; at least Alberich paid for the ring by the renunciation of love but Wotan seems to think it belongs to himself, by right.

> "Shall Alberich go free?" asks Loge

> "Set him free" says Wotan

> "Slink away home" commands Loge

But as soon as he is free Alberich's first words strike fear into Loge's heart.

> "As by curse the ring came to me so shall this ring be accursed for ever. Neither triumph nor contentment shall reward the ring holder, but only envy, care and death. He who possesses it shall be consumed with care. Those who do not possess it shall be gnawed with envy. Its owner shall guard it in endless fear and shall long for death until I hold it again in my hands.

Take the ring Wotan and, with it, take my curse."

Alberich has placed a terrible curse[10] on the ring which Wotan's treacherous behaviour can only strengthen. Loge is desperately worried but, already, Wotan is too engrossed in the ring to care.

Chapter 4: Donner

He likes to think of himself as a man of action but, like a child's, Donner's thoughts reach crescendos of emotion: ending in dramatic and often violent relief.

Before Wotan's return from Nibelheim Donner could be heard muttering away to himself.

"The air is oppressive. Since Freya went it is so dark. Not the honest darkness of a storm but the darkness of approaching gloom. What are they doing with Freya? How could I- how could we - carry on without her? I need to go to their lair. I can't stand this dark, this not knowing, this jealousy. I'll hit out,

DONNER

I need a storm, a fight, a conclusion. The castle may be well built but Freya's apples give better protection. I will go to their lair and deal with them. Whose footsteps are those? Aah! The giants are back. Where's Freya? There! Already the place seems lighter. Already I feel strong. Is she unharmed? I can't see. She looks frightened. What have they done to her? With one swing of my hammer I could— but the spear is against me. Why should I be so beholden to that spear? One day perhaps I can do away with these impediments that rule our lives. And now Wotan's here with the new ring on his finger. That swirling of the mists means he is dissatisfied. I must be careful. Why is he in this mood? That foul cursing of Alberich's meant little to him, surely. What's that? Now Fasolt is not sure he wants to lose Freya and is singing of his love for her. What an idea. What a fool. My hammer twitches in my hand. Fafner wants the gold piled around Freya so that Fasolt can no longer see her. What idiots giants are. How can we demean ourselves like this? But it seems Wotan's deal must stand so I suppose I must help. Soon they shall feel the weight of my hammer. Soon the air will clear. Pile up the gold. If those giants don't stop shouting that they need more and more gold they will regret it. It's so shameful for Freya, so demeaning for us. Pile it up. That's all the gold around Freya. What's that Fasolt saying now? There is a small chink through which he can see Freya's hair. Yes yes there it is, her wonderful soft golden *hair! How can these giants be allowed to so much as lay their eyes on it? Well done Wotan, throwing that helmet over the gap, but he doesn't seem too pleased to lose it. Now what? Fasolt saying he can still see her eyes and he can't tear himself away from her while he can still see them and Fafner pointing to the ring on Wotan's finger. Yes there is the glitter of her eyes. Well, I can understand what Fasolt feels, dolt as he is. How he must yearn to have someone beautiful and so in love with life as to grow those apples. Aah! Fafner still pointing to the ring to fill the gap. I have never seen Wotan so furious. Loge saying that the ring should go back to the Rhinemaidens as he promised, and Wotan shouting that Loge's promise does not bind him. Loge turning to fire and back again, the mists swirling. Wotan raving about the power of the ring and how he must keep possession of it. Fafner saying that the giants will keep Freya instead and Freya crying. She's crying!"*

"Give up the ring Wotan!"

"But perhaps I could stop all this, if I had the ring instead. Something is happening. Everything seems to be going black. I should have the ring! Of course, it's obvious I should have it. Me. the God of war and thunder. With the hammer and the ring I could settle everything. Everyone will do my bidding. That's what we need. But, but - everything is black."

Later Donner learnt that all the Gods became lost in black mists and felt that they were losing their senses. Through the mists, just as he was finally refusing to give up the ring, Wotan had a vision, which the other

Gods only partially shared. As Asgard turned dark, a blue light shone from out of the rocks. The winds fell silent and in the centre of the light, as if risen from the rock, stood a tall thin female figure shrouded in waist length hair. Her body looked young but her face was lined with wisdom and care. Wotan immediately recognised her as Erda, the mother of the earth and of all things: and he felt an immediate and great love for her.

"Yield it, Wotan," She sang. "Yield it.
A dark day is coming for the Gods. Flee the ring's curse. Disaster lies in its might.
Escape from its curse.
Its possession dooms you"

"What woman warns me of this?" Asks Wotan

"All that was and all that will be I see. Great danger calls me to this place. Give it up Wotan."

Slowly, despite Wotan's desperate attempts to make her stay, she disappears back into the rock, proclaiming that Wotan should reflect in fear and dread. Wotan now has to make a decision that many in this tale have to take. A decision between love: putting others before one's own desires, and power, which is usually the opposite.

"Heed her." Shouts Froh as the black mists begin to dissolve.

Wotan is convinced and throws the ring into the gap with relief.

" To me, Freya, you shall be free, bring us our youth again. Take your ring, Giants"

While the Gods embrace, Fafner greedily starts to gather up the gold and the Gods watch in awe as the ring's curse takes immediate effect.

"Hey leave me my share!" shouts Fasolt

"You cared more for the maid than the gold," booms Fafner "Left to you we would have no gold and therefore I shall take the greater part."

Fasolt calls him a thief and asked the Gods to judge. Wotan turns away but Loge suggests to Fasolt that he should keep just the ring.

Fasolt agrees.
"Away Fafner, I shall keep the ring, was it not given because I could see Freya's glance?"

Fafner is furious and attacks Fasolt with his club, shouting,
" Don't touch the ring. It is mine. Just gloat on Freya's glance, for you will not see the ring again."

A mighty but brief struggle occurs between the two giants. Fafner has the advantage of surprise and Fasolt soon falls dead from a fierce blow from Fafner's club. The Gods are horrified as Fafner strolls off with the hoard.

" The ring's curse is fearful." Moans Wotan, feeling chastened. "I must commune again with Erda."

Fricka is already jealous of Erda and distracts Wotan by declaring that he is now free to enter Valhalla and enjoy the luxury within. " But the work was paid with such evil wage" muses Wotan, brooding on whether the already corrupted fortress will be enough for his needs. His encounter with Erda has made him

DONNER

thoughtful. He feels unable to control his own fate: bound by Fricka's laws and Loge's lies, he is shackled and careworn. To be a God is to dispense with freedom. Perhaps it need not be like that. There may be a way out of trickery, compromises and deceit. Would a race of innocent heroes, free from compromise, help achieve his ends? Could an innocent hero, free to think for himself, succeed where the Gods fail?[11]

Donner, though, is exulted: thieving, fighting, captives, curses, murder, love, loss and redemption of Freya, all combine to allow him to swing his hammer with great effect.

> "Hovering clouds come, lightening and thunder
> sweep the heavens. Help me brother! Point the way"

Donner commands the mists to come to him. The mists darken and a massive thunderstorm is upon them all. Soon the black disperses to reveal Froh's best handiwork. A massive rainbow[12] provides a bridge to the gates of the fortress of Valhalla.

> " The bridge is light but firm. Walk it undaunted as
> it carries you home." Donner cries in triumph.

Donner's antics revive and amuse Wotan. He praises the evening light and says that all that he now desires is to wake up tomorrow in his new Valhalla. "Follow me. Come wife, live with me in Valhalla." He cries, as he ascends the bridge.

The Gods follow him happily, except for Loge, who walks as far as the base of the bridge and muses to himself.

> "They think themselves great but their dealings are shameful. Four times I tried to persuade Wotan to return the ring to the Rhinemaidens. I am tempted to return to fire and burn down their useless fortress. Who knows, maybe one day I shall."

As the Gods ascend the bridge, in the stillness after the storm, from far below the song of the Rhinemaidens can just be heard.

> "Rhinegold, rhinegold, how brightly you shone.
> Return the gold, return the gold to the river children."

"Cease that noise." Shouts Wotan from the bridge. "Loge shut them up!"

The Rhinemaidens continue:
> "Would that the treasure were glittering yet in the deep.
> It was tender and true in the water but false and base are all who revel above."

> "Hear Wotan's commands" spits Loge. "The gold shall not gleam upon you again. You should be basking in bliss in the wondrous radiance of the Gods instead."

As the Gods enter Valhalla for the first time, Donner wonders why Loge always seems to spoil things.

Chapter 5: The Volsungs

As Fricka feared it was not long before Wotan became restless in his new home.

Increasingly he appeared to be haunted by his imagined enemies and his own thoughts. Events outside the world of the Gods obsessed him and the runes on his spear depressed him. Wotan became elusive as he began to use all the powers at his disposal to disperse his demons. Time became his plaything; he would appear unsought in different places in different guises as if trying out the various personas who might help him with his problem. He sought out Erda and with a combination of patience, soft caresses and intimate persistence warmed her body and aroused her to the degree that she revealed more of her store of knowledge than she might have wished. She bore him nine daughters, who became known as The Valkyries.[13] Wotan brought these sisters to Valhalla and trained them to build an army of heroes to help protect the fortress. On their flying horses, encased in heavy armour, they would overlook human conflict and choose out suitable warriors who had fallen in battle.

In their youthful zeal the girls enjoyed galloping through the air, choosing out the most courageous and powerful mortals to whom they could promise semi-immortality in Valhalla. This was not delicate work and the girls were well equipped for the job. Animal-like in their abilities and senses, they could scour the battlefield from on high with eagle-like eyes. Their hearing and sense of smell were as acute as those of any hunting animal. More than strong enough to throw the largest hero over their saddles they thought little of bundling severed limbs into their cavernous saddlebags. To those creatures of earth who could see them, they were a fearsome sight. No giant or dwarf would interfere with their work and looting of battlefield spoils would be unthinkable before these flying amazons had taken their pickings. Scavengers, too stayed away for several days, discouraged by the strong odour they left behind, which many likened to that of a bear. Yet they were deemed to serve the heroes of Valhalla well. Valhalla became legendary amongst the men of the north and to die a hero's death in order to be chosen became the aim of many. These activities helped Wotan to forget his problems as he revelled in the action and in the fickle praise of men. He would call the sisters his wish-maidens when they carried out his commands perfectly. Chief and eldest of the Valkyries was one who went by the name of Brünnhilde. She was as full of youthful energy as her sisters but possessed many of the qualities of her mother, which boded well for her future wisdom and insight. Wotan had given her Grane, the best of the flying horses. She seemed able to anticipate Wotan's wishes by instinct and more than once performed the required actions before he had even formulated his own desires. Her sense of smell was particularly well developed. She often attributed her remarkable insight to this sensitivity, claiming to be able to smell out the best heroes and Wotan's requirements, even before he

THE VOLSUNGS

knew them himself. Wotan had always been fond of Brünnhilde and their relationship strengthened as Brünnhilde matured. So close had they become that sometimes they seemed sometimes to be different aspects of the same person. As might be expected, Erda's talented daughter was not a favourite with Fricka.

Another of Wotan's activities was the spawning of the Volsung[14] race, whose wolf-like activities are probably the origin of the werewolf legends. The mother of this race is unknown but she is known to have had unusual snake-like marking in her eyes - a characteristic trait which was passed down the generations. Emerging from his forest home at night, Wotan enjoyed assuming the appearances or near-appearances of a wolf. A number of offspring resulted from his liaison with this woman but, towards the end of this stage in Wotan's life, observers in the forest noted that there were two other half-human, half-wolf forms accompanying him. These creatures sometimes seemed to merge with the father to form a single one-eyed wolf-like creature and at other times were three clearly definable human entities. The human forms persisted and differentiated into twins: male and female, Siegmund and Sieglinde. As they grew, their memories of their wolf-like existence faded. Their lives in the forest became increasingly tough and painful, as their father seemed to be training them for some future ordeal. One wet afternoon when Siegmund and his father were scouring the forest they came home to find their home burnt by robbers. Siegmund's mother lay dead and his twin sister and constant companion had obviously been taken by force. With his father he pursued the robbers, killing many, but, looking round during the battle, Siegmund suddenly realised that his father too had gone and only a wet wolf skin ground into the mud of the forest floor remained.

Sieglinde had been taken by raiders and had been rapidly married off, at a considerable price, to a warlord who commanded a large tract of the forest some considerable distance away. He had no idea of her origins but was happy that she was young and attractive. She knew the ways of the forest and represented new blood in a region that had little contact with the outside world. Little else mattered to Hunding once Sieglinde had become his property. As befitted his station he inhabited a large wood–built house or small fortress, built round a massive live ash tree that grew in the centre of the hall.[15] At his grand wedding to Sieglinde an uninvited guest had arrived. He was covered in a dark cloak with a large brimmed hat pulled down over one eye. The guests were afraid of him but Sieglinde caught his eye and felt she recognised him as he gave her a slight nod. The stranger had said little but, with great show, managed to bury a sword up to its hilt in the ash tree. So well driven in was the sword that Hunding, who was a very powerful figure, was unable to remove it, nor could anyone else who visited the house. Sieglinde recalled that her brother had once told her that their father would, one day, leave a sword for him in his time of dire need. This sword was Sieglinde's only consolation as the years wore on. For she heard no more of her brother and was soon resolved to swapping her life of freedom in the forest for one of loneliness, drudgery and near slavery in Hunding's gloomy fortress.

Although life in the forest without shelter was hard, Siegmund had little trouble in surviving but, bereft of his twin, he felt incomplete. He sought companionship at the forest edge but proved incapable of compromise with his fellow men. As a semi–God, human frailty mystified him and he constantly felt compelled to interfere where wiser men would merely observe.

Many feared the rumours of his origins and were concerned about the markings in his eyes. Those men and women who did befriend him would eventually give up and shun him, feeling it was impossible to match up to his standards and accept his constant criticism. Only his considerable physical prowess and wolf-like cunning kept him safe from those who would remove him from the forest altogether.

We are at Hunding's house and the weather is foul. A gross black cloud darkens the evening prematurely and the thunder shakes even the massive ash tree as Sieglinde clears the hearth and awaits the return of her husband. The windows are heavily shuttered. The only light comes from the fire and a few small candles. A long table sits in front of the hearth and a few hunting trophies hang from the walls. The floor is of dried earth. The oak door suddenly blows open but, instead of her husband, a soaked and wounded stranger staggers in. He throws himself down by the fire, declaring that he can go no further and must rest where he lies. Sieglinde immediately offers him water and mead and tends his wounds, telling him that her husband will soon arrive and that he must stay in this house for the night. As the stranger recovers he announces that he must leave. Sieglinde asks him why this is necessary and who is pursuing him that he has to leave. He replies,

> "It is bad luck pursues me wherever I go;
> Bad luck approaches wherever I stop.
> May it keep away from you, good woman."

But Sieglinde is not afraid of bad luck.

> "Then stay here!
> You cannot bring bad luck into a house where bad luck thrives."

Hunding arrives; he is also tired, and after hearing about his new guest roughly demands that Sieglinde serves a meal to the men. They all sit at the table and Hunding asks the stranger his name and how he came to be in this house on such a night, but the stranger merely announces that he has travelled for many hours and has little idea of where he is or from where he has travelled.

> "Well." Says Hunding, "If you will not tell me your story then perhaps you will tell my wife for she is clearly greedy to question you."

Hunding is anxious to know more about this stranger for he has noticed a resemblance between the stranger and his own wife. This is particularly notable in the snake-like marking in their eyes – a feature of his wife that he has frequently wondered about. It is also clear to Hunding that there is strong mutual attraction between the two of them. The twins however have not yet recognised each other. Perhaps this is not surprising, given the changes wrought by the ravages of time and hardship and the circumstances in which they find themselves.

The stranger tells his story in mournful song. With some circumspection he tells of his difficulties: of how he calls himself woeful, although he would prefer to call himself cheerful: of how he was brought up in the forest with his parents and twin sister and of the dreadful day when the home was burnt down. Sieglinde, of course, now recognises him and asks about his father but Siegfried can only tell her about the wolf skin and goes on to tell them about his life since.

THE VOLSUNGS

"I left the woodland and was drawn to men and women.
But whenever I sought friends, or courted women: I was always unpopular.
Bad luck dogged me.
Whatever I thought right, seemed wrong to others.
Whatever seemed wrong to me, seemed correct to them.
I met disfavour wherever I went.
If I hankered for happiness, I stirred up misery.
So I had to be called "Woeful".
Woe is all I possess."

Hunding muses that much of this is likely to be Siegmund's own fault and asks again how he came to be here, wounded and unarmed. This time Siegmund tells them that he met with a child who cried to him for protection, as she was being forced into marriage with an older man she did not love. Siegmund decided to help her and soon found himself in a fierce battle with her oppressors and amongst the slain were the girl's two brothers. The girl became distraught and had thrown herself over the bodies of her brothers, blaming Siegmund for their deaths and refusing to move. Siegmund stood by the bodies and defended her against increasing numbers, until his sword and shield were broken. He was forced to flee into the forest as the crowd fell on the girl and killed her.

Hunding nods and shows little surprise. When Siegmund is finished, he announces that he had been called on to defend that family's honour. He had arrived too late but now he was the leader of Siegmund's pursuers. The rules of forest hospitality forbid Hunding to take any action overnight but come the morning, the pursuit must be finalised and Hunding warns Siegmund to arm himself for tomorrow. He locks the fortress so that there is no escape and bellows at Sieglinde to leave the room and prepare his night drink. He leaves Siegmund reflecting on the danger of his situation.

Siegmund is no stranger to fear but has the true bravery of being able to face his fear. He is trapped in the house of a well armed and powerful man who has servants and vassals to do his bidding and who fully intends to kill him in the morning. He recalls that his father had promised to leave him a sword in a time of great need and, as he does so, he notices a reflection from the fire high up in the tree. While he wonders what this is, Sieglinde enters the room and tells him that she has put a sleeping draught in Hunding's drink. She tells him of her own origins and a rapturous reunion soon follows. Pointing out the sword she recounts the story of how it got there. As she does so, the storm outside stops raging, calmness returns and early morning sunlight seeps through the shutters. Siegmund gaily climbs the tree and, seemingly without effort, removes the sword from the trunk. Holding it aloft he names it 'Nothung' (Needed). There is, it seems, no immediate need for him to face Hunding for, as soon as the sword is removed, the window shutters and the massive oak door burst open to reveal a fine spring dawn. The two lovers rush towards the hills to consummate their joy and complete their destiny. Released from their individual torments, in their joy of meeting once more, they soon completely abandon themselves to their forbidden and uninhibited love. The morning sun had not yet cleared a layer of ground mist when they came across the stream that marked the boundary of the forest and the foothills. Steam was rising from the river as Sieglinde deported herself seductively on the bank and joyously abandoned her body to the attentions and lusty shouts of her brother.[16]

"Wife and sister, you will be to your brother.

So let the Volsung blood increase."

Wotan was well pleased with his work. Here, at last, was a hero, greater than any of those in Valhalla, who would be able to achieve his aims. Wotan expected Siegmund to kill Fafner, obtain the gold and, in his innocence, be free of the curse. Then perhaps he could help Wotan rid himself of the obligations of the spear. Wotan was sitting on his throne in the great Hall at Valhalla. A huge space with walls apparently stretching out to infinity disappeared into the darkness behind him. There were many heavy doors, all closed. The roof was lined with shields and the walls hung with spears. The throne was of massive dark carved oak. At his feet lay a wolf, and an eagle stood at his shoulder. Overhead three ravens circled untiringly, waiting for Wotan's orders. Through this space and through those doors Wotan's mind could travel at will. Each door opened on to a different aspect. One door only did he find difficult to open. Only on the edge of his dreams, just before wakening, could he enter a space of variable dimensions, supported by the decaying roots of the world ash tree. The walls and floor were of dry soil and the ceiling of jagged rock. Here amongst the smell of sleep and earth, her cold body merged with the soil and ever reluctant to respond, he would find Erda. Another door, entering onto a series of warm mountain springs, was Brünnhilde's own. Here could she escape her loud sisters, giggling over their latest fashionable hero. Here could she stand in front of the mirror she had placed on a rocky cleft and slyly, slowly, remove her heavy armour, piece by heavy piece, as if casting off the responsibilities of her post. Her helmet too could she remove and allow her hair to flow and caress her shoulders. Here could she mask the musky smell of the sulphurous springs by practiced use of the plants that grew there. Judicious scattering of crushed herbs and petals onto the waters of the chosen spring and the burning of well chosen barks, produced scents to match her mood. Here could she lower herself into the warm scented waters and allow the small waterfalls and deep powerful obliging eddies to massage her body and here could she dream of perfect, powerful and gentle heroes; strong enough to pierce her armour but, unfortunately, not yet born.

Summoning up Brünnhilde, Wotan tells her to watch over the forthcoming battle between Hunding and Siegmund and to ensure a win for Siegmund. Hunding he had no use for in Valhalla. Brünnhilde happily agrees to do his wishes but warns him that he still has a violent storm to face in order to reconcile his actions as she has seen Fricka appearing over the horizon in her chariot and heading for her usual door. With this, she hastens away to carry out Wotan's instructions. Wotan realises that he must finally consider some reasoned arguments about his behaviour and faces a painful internal dialogue between reason and his own wishes. He knows that a period of depression is the likely consequence.

Fricka complains bitterly that Wotan is avoiding her and is deluding himself over the effectiveness of his actions. She then points out the immorality of the situation. She has received a plea from Hunding, that Wotan's assistance to Siegmund has been an attack on the holy institution of marriage. Wotan easily deals with this by pointing out that the marriage was a forced one and therefore unholy. Fricka feels on stronger grounds when she declares her outrage at the incestuous nature of the twins' relationship "When did such a thing happen before?" She cries.

Wotan is ready with an emotional argument.

THE VOLSUNGS

"It has happened today. And you should learn from it.
It must be clear to you that these two are in love.
So listen to sensible advice.
Since their sweet content will reward you for your blessing,
Smile on love and bless Siegmund and Sieglinde's union.
For love is above the law."

This releases a long invective from Fricka, releasing all her pent up frustration and, to Wotan's relief, gets her off the main track of her argument.

She complains that there is no point in discussing the sanctity of marriage with Wotan for he breaks his vows repeatedly anyway and never comes home. He is working against everything a God should stand for, breaking up all he has achieved, running round in the forest in a ridiculous wolf's garb creating semi-wild creatures, which are no more than projections of his own self and, as for those Valkyries galloping round after heroes and – and – and.

Happily, Wotan falls back on his mysterious ways argument. He says that he is a believer in trying out new ways and that Fricka is far too conventional. He requires a hero, free of divine help, who can help him out of his current crisis. Unfortunately for Wotan, Fricka becomes rational again.

"What marvels could heroes perform
that Gods are unable to do?
By whose favour can men act?
Who inspires men's bravery?
Who lights up the fools' eyes?
Through your goading they have their aspirations.
Only under your protection they appear strong."

Wotan protests that he has not protected Siegmund and Fricka has him.

> "Then do not shelter him today." She shouts triumphantly
> "Take away the sword."

> "But Siegmund himself won it in adversity." Says Wotan.

> "You created the adversity for him,
> just as you created the flashing sword."

Wotan is defeated. Finally he is forced to face reality. Siegmund cannot be considered to be free of his help and any actions undertaken by Siegmund would only be those of himself. Far from helping Wotan out of his difficulties, this is likely to only increase them. Sadly he agrees that he will not help "the Volsung". Fricka says that "the Valkyrie" must not help him either. Wotan tries to argue that Brünnhilde should make up her own mind but is soon defeated as Fricka points out that she only obeys his orders.

Fricka is satisfied that her own lawful position has been re-established and that decency will be observed.

> "Today the Valkyrie's shield shall protect your eternal wife's sacred honour.
> Men will laugh at us, our power will be lost and we Gods will disappear, if today, in a decent and respectable manner, my rights are not upheld by that bold girl.
> The Volsung shall die for my honour.
> Do I have Wotan's oath on it?"

THE VOLSUNGS 53

"Take my oath!" growls Wotan miserably over his shoulder as he goes off to the stables to suppress his own desires and give Brünnhilde her new instructions.

Brünnhilde greets him with the remark that, as Fricka looks happy, the outcome of the argument must have been bad. Wotan tells Brünnhilde he is in despair and she asks him for the details. "After all" She says. "Who am I, if not your own will? Telling me your secrets is the same as admitting them to yourself."

Depressed and debating with himself, as much as with Brünnhilde, Wotan enumerates his difficulties and makes his mid-life confession.

> "In my youth so much did I long for power that I acted dishonestly, Tempted by Loge, I made alliances which allowed evil to flourish quietly and unseen. But absolute power eluded me for I could never abandon love. Alberich, though, cursed love and the gold became his. Although I tricked him out of the ring, I could not use it effectively without foregoing love and so, when Erda warned me against it, I gave up the ring in payment for Valhalla. Erda's knowledge and wisdom were clearly vital to me so I sought her out and forced her give up her secrets. She bore me yourself and your eight sisters. All I wanted was to avert the end of the Gods, as she warned me that enemies would soon overpower us. That is why I needed your heroes, whom I bound to me with deceitful treaties."

"I have brought you many heroes, why despair now?"

"Erda also told me that the end of the Gods will come through Alberich. I do not fear him unless he

steals back the ring, for only then could he could bring defeat upon the Gods.
The ring is guarded by Fafner who has no real use for it but I cannot take it from him as I gave it to him in payment and yet more treaties would be forfeited. I am enslaved by my treaties.
Only one person could do what I cannot: a stranger to the Gods, a hero free of favours who, unprompted, could do the deed and take the ring from Fafner.
How can I create a free agent whom I have never protected and, by defying me, will be most dear to me?
With disgust I find only myself in everything I create."

"But the Volsung is free."

"No I trained him in the woods. I gave him his sword. I provoked him to boldness. I defrauded myself again.
I touched Alberich's ring and, although I gave it away, the curse is still with me. The person whom I cherish must die in battle with Hunding.
All I want now is the end, the end.
The end for which Alberich is already working, for although he has forsworn love, he has seduced a woman with money. Already his offspring is stirring in her womb and he will have someone to help carry on his work. Yet I, who wooed for love, cannot beget a free man.
Take my blessing son of the Nibelung and take my divinity. It is worthless"

"What must I do?" asks Brünnhilde.

"Fight for Fricka, not me and ensure that Siegmund dies"

THE VOLSUNGS 55

"You love Siegmund, you have taught me to love him. My senses tell me that you do not wish this. Your orders are two faced."

"Do not disobey my orders for my wrath will be terrible and your courage would fail you. My orders are that Siegmund shall die."

"Then I must in sorrow forsake my friend." Groans Brünnhilde as she rides off to the battle.

Whilst the Gods were thus deciding their fates, the twins, after thier brief interlude of joy, were running for their lives from Hunding's dog pack in the high mountains above his forest. Spring had not yet penetrated this high and it was pouring with rain. There was scarcely a path. They were both covered in mud and badly scratched by the undergrowth. Sieglinde particularly was suffering: feverish and exhausted she was close to raving. Abandoning her marriage, indulging in incest and, she thought, bringing ruin on her brother were weighing heavily upon her. Breaking her own behavioural and moral rules had made her particularly vulnerable to Fricka's wrath.

"Let the wind blow away what I vilely gave to that hero.
Though he clasped me lovingly, though I found sublimest joy.
There soon came fear and terror, ghastly shame and disgrace."

Siegmund feels none of this but resolves to stand and fight, as Sieglinde clearly cannot continue. Sieglinde is highly sensitive to Fricka's intentions for, as she hears Hunding's horn, she begs one last kiss, foreseeing Siegmund's defeat and the shattering of his sword.

As Siegmund tends to the half conscious Sieglinde and waits for the battle, Brünnhilde appears to him. She tells him that only those who are about to die are able to see her and offers him a place in Valhalla. There he will see his father and all his needs will be satisfied. "Will I see Sieglinde there?" He asks. Brünnhilde tells him that she will need to stay on earth. His reply surprises her.

> "Then greet Valhalla for me.
> Greet Wotan and all the heroes.
> Greet the lovely wishmaidens too.
> I will not follow you to them."

Brünnhilde declares that when he dies in battle he will come to Valhalla anyway.

> "And who is going to fell me?"

> "Hunding." says Brünnhilde

Siegmund points out that he will need to be threatened with stronger foes than that and perhaps Brünnhilde can take Hunding to Valhalla instead. He reminds her of the power of his sword and Brünnhilde is forced to tell him that, he who made the sword intends to take away its power.

Siegmund understands and looks lovingly at his sister. "Do not frighten her." He says. "If I must betray her in battle then hell, not Valhalla, will hold me fast."

Brünnhilde is amazed and distraught.
> "Is she everything to you, this poor woman
> who, tired, wet and sorrowful, lies limp in your lap?"

Siegmund has heard enough.

THE VOLSUNGS

"So young and fair and dazzling you look,
but how cold and hard you must be.
If you can only scoff, then take yourself away."

This is too much for Brünnhilde. How can she carry out Wotan's orders to ensure the death of such a man? Orders, which she knew were not Wotan's genuine desires. Resolutely she sings out:

"Confide her protection to me.
Rely on your sword and wield it boldly.
The weapon will be true to you."

Hunding arrives out of the driving rain and threatens Siegmund with Fricka's wrath. To his credit, feeling safe in Fricka's protection, he calls off his dogs and followers and prepares for single-handed battle. Siegmund shouts defiance and, accompanied by lightening flashes and thunder from Donner's hammer, they rush at each other. Brünnhilde, unseen by Hunding, holds her shield in front of Siegmund and Hunding soon weakens as his sword thrusts are continuously deflected. At the climax of the battle, just as Siegmund is wielding Hunding's deathblow, Wotan makes a magical appearance and holds his spear in front of Nothung. Accompanied by the sound of a massive thunderclap, Nothung shatters on the spear, and it is Siegmund who falls dead, following Hunding's last despairing sword thrust. Shocked but mindful of her promise to protect Sieglinde, Brünnhilde scoops up the shattered sword, places Sieglinde on her horse and flees in haste from Wotan's wrath.

Wotan strikes Hunding dead with a contemptuous wave of his hand, suggesting to Hunding's soul that he should kneel before Fricka and tell her that Wotan has done her bidding. For a long time, he gazes sadly at

Siegmund's soaking body. Finally he looks up, his face flushed with anger and growls.

"And now Brünnhilde must face my punishment for her crime."

Chapter 6: Brünnhilde I

That part of Wotan which works by instinct, which enjoys uncontrolled hedonism and which he loves without inhibition must be set aside if Wotan is to succeed. She may be revived in wiser form but now Wotan's great need is to suppress his wayward offspring and, like all fathers before him, must be prepared to lose his daughter to a youthful upstart.

Brünnhilde flies towards the protection of her sisters. They are transporting dead heroes from a far off battle. As is usual after a battle they are full of life and energy and hysteria: shouting lustfully at each other as they fly back in formation. Gradually they begin to sense that something is amiss, their shouts become less boisterous and more hysterical as they near the agreed meeting place. Brünnhilde finds them there, high on a rocky mountaintop: a place that provides a lookout for miles around, with a clump of small trees and a nearby cave for shelter. As she flies towards them their fears are confirmed when they realise that it is a live woman and not a deceased male hero that she carries over her saddle. Brünnhilde quickly tells them what has happened and how she needs to hide from Wotan, whilst protecting Sieglinde. Sieglinde rouses herself and asks them not to plague themselves by worrying about her. All she wants to do now is die. Brünnhilde, however, has her reasons for protecting Sieglinde. Her instincts have detected that Sieglinde is pregnant and she tells Sieglinde that she must live in order to protect the child.

"A Volsung is growing in your womb."

Sieglinde is in a worse situation than Brünnhilde: her husband and her brother and father of her child are both dead. She is ill, and is lying on an unprotected mountaintop with no way of getting home. Even if she could get home, it seems unlikely that she could continue to live there. The wrath of a God is about to descend upon her, as well as upon Brünnhilde, and now, far from being happy to die, she is responsible for the future of her brother's baby.

"Protect me then." She cries.
"Protect a mother!" she pleads to the other
Valkyries

A massive storm is fast approaching and the sisters recognise that Wotan's wrath is not far off. They are too frightened of Wotan to help Sieglinde directly but agree that Brünnhilde will stay on the rock to face Wotan, whilst Sieglinde escapes on foot to the nearby forests. The Valkyries are worried that this is the same forest where Fafner lies in his cave. This is hardly a safe situation, but at least Wotan appears to avoid this forest.

Brünnhilde says a rapid goodbye to Sieglinde, reminds her to protect the sword fragments and tells her what name to give to her offspring. Sieglinde sets off towards the east and shouts a prophetic blessing to

BRÜNNHILDE 1

Brünnhilde that Sieglinde's gratitude shall bring her a reward.

The Valkyries gather in front of Brünnhilde to protect her from Wotan, who soon arrives demanding that they should not protect the lawbreaker. They summon up enough courage to ask what it is that Brünnhilde has done. Wotan replies,

> "No one but she knew my intentions, or my
> innermost thoughts.
> She was the fertile womb of my wishes.
> Now she has broken this sacred alliance.
> She has defied my will.
> She has scorned her master's orders.
> She has taken up arms against me.
> Though only my wishes brought her to life."

Brünnhilde comes forward to meet him.
> "Here I am, father:
> pronounce your punishment."

> "I do not punish you myself.
> You made your own punishment.
> I made you disposer of fates,
> but you disposed fate against me.
> I made you the inspiration of heroes,
> but you inspired the heroes against me.
>
> You are no longer my wish's agent.
> Your time as a Valkyrie is over.
> You are exiled from the company of Gods and
> immortals
> You are banished from my sight.
>
> Here on the mountain I shall confine you.
> In defenceless sleep I shall lock you.
> Any man who finds you can capture you."

To be under the control of the first man who finds her is the most terrible punishment the Valkyries can imagine. They plead with Wotan but he dismisses them.

> "Your faithless sister is banished from your company
> She will never ride again
> The flower of her youth will wither away.
> A husband will win her womanly favours.
> To this man she will belong thenceforward.
> She will sit by the fire and spin-
> the topic and butt of all jokers.
>
> Does her fate terrify you?
> Then fly from this lost soul.
> If any of you dare to dawdle beside her,
> if anyone disobeys me and clings to her in her sadness,
> that fool shall share her fate
> Now be off from here."

The Valkyries have no option but to leave Brünnhilde to her fate.

Brünnhilde is distraught but not entirely unrepentant,
> "Was it so shameful what I did?
> Look me in the eyes. Silence your rage. Control your anger.
> Consider why you have to abandon your favourite child and companion
> for did I not carry out your wishes"

> "Did I command you
> to fight for the Volsung?"

> "You did."

BRÜNNHILDE 1

"I reversed that command."

"Yes, but only when Fricka made you a stranger to your own intentions.
I am not clever, but I knew one thing - you loved the Volsung.
I knew your dilemma because my eyes are yours
When Wotan is at war, I guard his back,
I saw what you could not see-
I heard the sounds of the Volsung's lament.
I learnt of his unbounded love, his terrible sorrow,
I saw his magnificent defiance.
I knew that you loved him for he breathed love into my own heart
So was I not faithful to you inwardly when I disobeyed your command."

Brünnhilde's admission of love for the Volsung, reminds Wotan of his own and her mention to him of the closeness between them breaks through his resolve. Suddenly they are closer than ever before but no longer are they father and daughter. They are like lovers who have to part for the sake of their own futures.

Wotan sadly confesses his agony and jealousy and appears to admit to suicidal thoughts.

"You did what I wanted so much to do.
Did you imagine love's bliss was so easily attained?
Just as you were sweetly enjoying the joys of bliss,
And your heavenly emotions made you smile as you drank the draught of love.
My distress mingled with gall and agony were such that I would end my endless sadness"

"My own instinct told me only one thing." Replies Brünnhilde. "To love what you loved."

Wotan takes her in his arms and caresses her, clearly now distraught that he has to leave her. She leans against him and softly murmurs in his ear:

> "Do not dishonour an everlasting part of you,
> My disgrace would disgrace yourself.
> You would demean yourself if you saw people mock
> and laugh at me.
>
> If I must leave Valhalla,
> if I must be subordinated to a domineering man:
> then let no cowardly boaster have me as his prize.
> He who wins me must not be worthless.
> Wotan, I know that a great hero will be born to the Volsung race."

"Hold your tongue about the Volsung race!" Shouts Wotan angrily.
"When I gave you up I gave them up too."
Never ask me to protect the woman,
still less the fruit of her loins."

But Brünnhilde's instincts have not failed her and she carries on to tell him that Sieglinde has kept the remains of Nothung. She smiles and says

> "Let my sleep be protected by terrors that scare,
> so that only a fearless unrestrained hero
> may one day find me here on the rock."

"You ask too much."

> "Then destroy your child, who claps your knees,
> trample on your favourite, crush the girl,
> let all trace of her body be destroyed by your spear.
> Or let fire blaze up; let it burn round the rock with flaring flames, let its tongues flicker

and its teeth devour any coward who rashly dares to approach the fearsome rock."

Wotan can only relent and calls upon Loge to surround the rock with fire proclaiming:

> "Whosoever fears the tip of my spear
> shall never pass through the fire."

Softly he lays Brünnhilde down.

> "If I must reject you and may not greet you lovingly again;
> if you may no longer ride beside me nor bring me mead at table;
> if I must lose you whom I loved, the laughing joy of my eyes:
> then a bridal fire shall burn for you, as it never burned for any bride!
> Let it scare the fainthearted.
> Let cowards run away from Brünnhilde's rock!
> For only one shall win the bride;
> one who is freer than I, the God!
>
> Your eyes
> That bright pair of eyes that often I fondled with smiles,
> when the lust of battle won you a kiss,
> That radiant pair of eyes that often in tempests blazed at me,
> when hopeful yearning burned up my heart,
> when for worldly joy my desires longed
> for the last time let them delight me today
> with farewell's last kiss!"

Brünnhilde closes her eyes and with tender kisses on her lips, feels him firm against her.

Wotan my father-lover you have realised your destiny, your true self, your great love. We are one. I am your wish maiden.

She feels her breastplate being lifted away. Blocking out all sensations except the thrill of tightening to his touch she relaxes to finally, ecstatically, yield and fuse with him.[17]

At last, at last. But something has changed. A new smell, a young smell, a forest smell and, something else - Fear! Wotan is afraid of me!

She sits up and opens her eyes to find that Wotan has changed his appearance: still handsome and strong, but young, and he has both eyes. She too feels changed. Amused she smiles tenderly and looks around at her faithful Grane, standing under the trees.

The trees are taller.

Chapter 7: Brünnhilde 2

Hail to the world, Hail to this glorious day. Wotan, what a trick you played. Now I must teach this boy.

"Blessed hero! Conquering light!
If you but knew how I have always loved you.
You were my thought. You were my care.
I fed your tender being before you were begotten;
even before you were born my shield protected you:
so long have I loved you.

No! No! my boy I am not your sleeping mother. She will not come back to you.
I am your very self.[18]
What you do not know, I know for you.
I had a secret which I could not think of. I could only feel it.

You are my secret. I fought, strove and struggled, and I defied Wotan for you."

But my helmet no longer protects me
He has cut my breastplate's shining steel in two with his sword.
If he takes me now, my defences will be stripped. I shall no longer be a Valkyrie; perhaps I shall lose all my wisdom.
I will be exposed and unprotected. Already I feel a weak, defenceless woman!
Terror stalks me.

"O lover! Glorious being! Wealth of the world!
Life of the earth! Laughing hero!
Leave me in peace.
Do not come to me,
Do not overcome me with your overwhelming force, do not destroy your beloved!
As I was Wotan's will and Wotan's protection so I can be yours if you will leave me be. Together as one we can face the joys and terrors of the world and you will find yourself a loving wife. Look deep within yourself and find me there.
So if you do not touch me, ever bright and happy will you smile
Know yourself and let me be: do not destroy what is your own."

It is no use. He is confused, he does not understand.
He loves the light in my eyes, the stirring of my breath.
He is bound to me and is finding his courage again.
His lips burn with passionate thirst on my mouth and the flames that were round my rock now blaze within him. He takes what he can see and wisdom eludes him.

But just to look at him makes my senses swoon, my reason reels, and my eyes dim.
Must my wisdom wither?
We are lost in lust and love.

So be it. Awaken, then Brünnhilde! You are a woman now. Laugh and live in sweetest delight!

> "O Lover I have always been yours! Be mine, be mine, be mine!
> What you will be, be today!
> If my arms enfold you and hold you tight,

if my breast beats wildly against yours,
if our eyes kindle, and we breathe each other's breath,
eye to eye, mouth to mouth,
Then gone would be the burning doubt."

*Divine peace floods my being,
purest light blazes in the glow:
the wisdom of heaven flees from me,
chased away by the joy of love!
Lover, lover do you not see me?
As my eyes devour you, are you not blinded?
As my arms enfold you, do you not catch fire from me?
As my blood surges like a flood towards you,
do you not feel its raging fire?
Lover, do you not fear
this wild, passionate woman?*

"O childlike hero!
O sublime boy!
Laughing, I must love you,
laughing, I will bear my blindness;
laughing let us ruin,

laughing let us perish!"

Farewell, Valhalla's glittering world!
Let your proud fortress fall to dust!
Farewell, resplendent pomp of the Gods!
This boy will put an end to you. And I am glad.
Brünnhilde lives, Brünnhilde laughs!

Her lover knows only joy but has already learnt that joy is temporary.
    "She is forever mine,
    my inheritance, my own, my one and all.
    Radiant love brings laughing death!"

Chapter 8: Mime

THIS was undoubtedly the greatest challenge to his skill that Mime[19] had come across: a broken blade of a metal so hard that he was unable to reforge it.

Since he had obtained the sword Mime had converted a cave in the Eastern forest into a smithy. He had arranged the rocks in the cave into a suitably large forge and had fashioned a massive bellows out of skins. Many times had he tried to rejoin the pieces but the blade had always defeated him. Siegfried had been made any number of swords but, ever since he was able to pick them up, the boy had been able to smash them with one blow. Mime knew there was only one sword that could help carry out the purpose Mime expected of the boy and that sword lay wrapped up on the ground of their cave in pieces.

Siegfried had been difficult from the start: foolish, headstrong, determined and immensely strong and

MIME

Mime was no longer able to control him. Watching him go off into the forest this morning Mime had realised that he was no longer a boy. As Siegfried wandered further and further into the forest Mime feared that there was not much time left before Siegfried met another being. That would be disastrous, for Mime had made sure that Siegfried had grown up knowing no-one except himself and Siegfried knew no fear.

Mime could not remember a time when he was not afraid. His first memories were of being both frightened and fascinated by the sounds, smells and bustle of the Smithy. He could recall his childish shock on meeting the living, breathing bellows. The glowing charcoal suddenly erupting into a roaring flame that might singe his face at any time. The huge chimney that he could walk right into, gaping black like the entrance to another, even darker, world. The vat of placid water, with its mirror-like sheen at the level of his eyes, which would suddenly boil and hiss in protest as the glowing sword blades violated its surface. The massive horses backing into the yard with their huge clumping feet able to crush him with a single misplaced step. The shouts and the sweat of the ostlers and master smiths of his childhood and the comforting rhythmic ring of hammering on the anvil. And finally the magic transformation of hard grey metal into a soft and completely different substance, pliable to the hammer, but glowing red for danger.

Soon he was pumping the bellows himself and watching in awe the transformation of metal from a base shape into tools, ornaments or weapons. At a young age he lost interest in the activities of his fellows, preferring the slow predictable pumping of the bellows to their wild unstable play and the violence of his brother. Although he was useful to the smiths, they were concerned about his complete obsession with their activities to the exclusion of all else. They did not like nor trust him, for he was unable to look them in the eye and was reluctant to talk. The boy was demanding and their work might be disrupted by his need for regularity and predictability. They never knew when he might fly into a rage if the pattern of work was altered. Often he would listen to the clink of the hammer on the anvil and appear to be hypnotised by the sound. He would pump the bellows in time but he might suddenly throw himself on the floor screaming if the smith who was hammering changed his rhythm. On such occasions he would be thrown out of the smithy but was always allowed back a few days later, being far too useful to be rejected permanently. Sometimes he could be heard muttering the same word over and over again or putting together some rhyming words that he would use as a rhythmic chant: a habit that he put to more poetic use in later life. During his apprenticeship, which in human terms was long indeed, he learnt his trade rapidly and soon surpassed his teachers in his abilities to produce the hardest alloys, the tightest chain mail and the finest jewellery. His fellow dwarf-smiths found it odd that, once he had produced an article to a level of perfection that might make them gasp, he immediately became disinterested in its subsequent use or disposal. At first he was interested in hard iron and weapon manufacture but, as this work came easier to him, he turned to the softest of metals. That metal which is the easiest to work but is most difficult to perfect. His skill with gold became legendary. He could beat out the thinnest gold leaf, and produce the most intricate ornaments, hammering away for many hours in his own characteristic perfect rhythm.

His obsessions and rages and fears led to problems and bullying from his peers. Lacking his brother's strength of character, if not his physical strength, he would immerse himself totally in his work and communicate only by pointing for his needs. His constant failure to recognise the requirements of others meant that mostly he was left alone. In later youth it was gold that saved him from becoming a total recluse. He noticed that many of the visitors to the smithy appeared to have a similar, though less obsessive, interest in the metal and, whilst they watched him working with gold, their faces might soften and their voices become kinder. At such times Mime's fear would leave him enough to allow him to talk about his work and eventually about other matters. Dwarfs, humans and the various creatures with whom his brother had dealings, including giants and dragon-like creatures, all appeared to share his interest. Through gold Mime eventually found a way of communicating with the world.

He had tried hard to get Siegfried to do his bidding. He was constantly reminding him how he had found him in the forest and brought him up in the cave, protecting him, keeping him warm and free from harm but, unfortunately, Mime was not a man who inspired love in others.

Mime's fear rises up a notch when a bear comes rushing into the cave and he is only slightly relieved to see that Siegfried is driving the bear before him. Laughing, Siegfried teases Mime with the bear for a short time and then sends it lumbering back into the forest. Siegfried seems to fill the cave: broader and taller and stronger than the bear, he is wearing the bear's brother's skin round his torso. Open faced, his grin is in proportion, and his roars of laughter and impromptu song are louder than any roars bears can produce. Untutored, Siegfried is clearly capable of happily destroying anything that happens to obstruct him. Round his neck is a large silver horn that Mime had fashioned for him.

> "Why do you treat me like this?" Whines Mime. "You are so thankless. Did I not bring you up from a whimpering babe, give you food and drink and make you toys and a horn? Look I still wear myself out for you. I have made you food and drink and here is another sword for you to try. It is wonderfully sharp."

But Siegfried is unimpressed and has an important question for Mime.

> "What matters how sharp it is when it is such a fragile pin! See how I can shatter it easily. Make me a proper sword Mime, if I am to carry out the valiant deed you prattle on about and kill these giants. You have taught me many things but you cannot teach me to love you. For you shamble and shuffle and slink about, crawling and nodding and blinking and squinting and all I want to do is take you by your nodding neck and make an end of you.
> Listen to me, as I go into the wood and blow my horn, I meet creatures there that are much dearer to me than you. As I watch the beasts of the forest, Mime, I see that the young have a mother and father. The birds are fed in the nest by two parents. You taught me this yourself. The deer has both a mother and father, even the savage wolves lie in pairs.
> Where is my mother Mime?"

"I am both your mother and your father" whimpers Mime.

> "I have seen that baby animals are like their parents and I doubt if you are even my father for I have seen my face in the stream and we are as alike as a frog and a fish. Must I get the truth from you by blows?

MIME

Where is my mother Mime?"

And so, punctuated with much protestation of how well he looked after the babe, Mime finally tells Siegfried about his mother. He says that he found Sieglinde in the woods, desperately ill and about to give birth. As she died, Sieglinde asked him to call the babe Siegfried and gave him Siegfried's father's broken sword to look after[20], stating that the sword had shattered in her husband's last battle. Siegfried is forlorn to hear that his mother died at his own birth but also delighted to learn that Mime is not his father. He challenges Mime to prove the story and Mime shows him the shattered remains of Nothung.

> " My father's sword! You have kept this from me all this time. With that sword I could swim like a fish, fly like a finch and float like the wind. I can't stand it here with you any longer. I am going back into the forest, where I can think about my mother. Weld this sword for me quickly, Mime, so I can leave this place and seek my proper home."

Mime tries once again to forge the sword but he knows that his hammer cannot conquer the steel and that no furnace fire can serve him.

He toils hard but soon is too tired to carry on and, perhaps he has fallen asleep, for out of the forest emerges an old man wearing a dark blue cloak, a hat with a large brim covering one eye and calling himself 'Wanderer'. Mime tries to send him away but he refuses to go and settles down on the hearth to talk companionably. Wanderer says that he has seen much and is able to give wise counsel to those who ask. He challenges Mime to the ancient game of three questions with the wager being their own heads.

Mime happily agrees and asks his three questions: which race dwells under the ground, which race dwells on the earth and which race dwells in the heavens.
The Wanderer responds with the correct answers. The Nibelung dwarfs, the giants and the Gods and, in doing so, reminds Mime about the Nibelungs, led by Black Alberich, the finding of the ring and Fafner's stifling possession of the gold. He carries on to describe the power of the Gods led by Wotan whom he chooses to call "Light Alberich". In a sterner mood the Wanderer suddenly strikes his spear on the ground, a clap of thunder is heard and now it is his turn to ask the questions.

"Which race does Wotan love the best yet treat most harshly?"
"The Volsungs!" shouts Mime in triumph and recounts the story of Siegmund and Sieglinde and the babe Siegfried.

"What sword shall Siegfried use to rid Fafner of his gold?" "Nothung!" cries Mime without hesitation. "The sword that was found in the ash tree and none could draw out save Siegmund."

"And who shall reforge this sword?" demands Wotan. But Mime does not know. He jumps up and begins to rave.

"The sword, the splinters, the steel, I wish I had never seen it. It has brought me nothing but pain and care. My hand cannot weld it. I am the wisest of smiths yet I fail in this task"

Wanderer suggests to Mime that perhaps it would have been wiser to have asked questions to which he needed to know the answers and announces.

"He who does not know fear shall forge the sword. I shall leave you to forfeit your head to him."

By now Mime is too frightened to take notice:
"Accursed light –
what flickers and flashes, what flutters and whirls,
what floats and flies, what glistens and glows,
what hisses and hums what growls and roars
what comes from the forest with gaping jaws.
The dragon, the dragon it comes for me."

But it is Siegfried who enters from the forest to find Mime, alone, hiding and trembling behind the anvil. As Siegfried demands the sword, Mime finally has to admit that he is unable to forge it and that only he who does not know fear will be able to do so. Siegfried asks Mime if he will teach him about fear but Mime is as unable to teach Siegfried to feel fear, as he is unable to teach him to love him. Mime poesies about the beating of the heart.

"The shivers and the shakes,
the glowing and sinking,
the burning and fainting,
the beating and quaking."

Siegfried laughs and is unable to recognise any of this. He asks who could teach him such delights. Mime recalls Wanderer's last comment and realises that he now has an interest in Siegfried learning fear, at an appropriate time. He tells Siegfried that there is a dragon not so far away that will certainly be able to teach him. Siegfried is delighted but first he must forge the sword. He pumps the bellows singing to himself of the three elements that constitute his work. He sings of the earth of the forest that brought forth the fine tree, which he felled to make the charcoal. He sings of the rivers from which he carried the water and finally he sings of the fire that made the charcoal and will melt the steel. Instead of welding the broken fragments he immediately files the whole sword down. Then with only a hint of the fine Nibelung six note rhythm, which he learnt from Mime, he hammers out the steel with coarse heavy blows that would have made the young Mime cry out in frustration and pain. Mime soon realises that, with his fearlessness and lack of guile, Siegfried will achieve what he had failed to do with all his experience and craft.

Mime then muses on how he can obtain the gold without forfeiting his head. He considers that with the sword Siegfried will be able to kill the dragon but the dragon will surely teach him fear. Mime decides that the way to obtain the ring is to kill Siegfried with a poisonous potion after the battle. He starts cooking and, while Siegfried sings of forging the sword, Mime sings of cooking up a strong soup. He goes on to boast joyfully of the power he will wield, how he will be Prince of the Nibelung and of his forthcoming revenge on Alberich.

In the midst of Mime's gloating, Siegfried suddenly raises up the newly forged sword and brings it crashing down on the anvil. The anvil splits into two and Mime is afraid once more.

Chapter 9: Fafner

As he plodded away after killing his brother Fafner was aware of a change. Birds were twittering more clearly and seemed to be trying to tell him something. Fafner was determined not to listen.

Perhaps he wanted Freya and her golden apples after all. Quite what he wanted her for was unclear, but mixed feelings of tenderness and of wanting to force her towards his own cave were competing with each other. He recognised that he had assumed some of his brother's character. This was most unwelcome. Fafner desired the gold but his plans for the gold were unsure. He did not value its beauty nor its value as ornament. He knew that gold could be used for exchange, for self-advancement, for the procurement of power and to change things as he wanted but Fafner had no time for any of this. Change was an anathema to him; to keep the gold safe, unchanging and intact was a virtue. He wanted it for its own sake and for an illusion of warmth the cold metal produced. He had first noticed this warmth a long time ago during his dealing with dwarfs and was not sure if it was real. Often he had wondered whether others could feel it. He piled up the gold safely in his cave and thought. His thoughts were slow but troubled. He recognised a new desire for Freya and the warmth of contact with other creatures; desires which he began to think of as his 'Fasolt tendencies'. The more he tried to ignore them, the more they nagged his dreams. He even considered giving in to them. Perhaps there was a giantess who might share his cave? But he had always seen such thoughts as weakness and, besides, Fafner was not sure how to handle a giantess and did not quite know what would be expected of him. In truth he felt a little afraid. Finally he realised that he would have to share his gold hoard and that was unthinkable. No, he would put aside his Fasolt tendencies and guard his gold. Tender thoughts were of no use to him. Despite this decision, his dreams did not leave him and his thoughts were rarely restful.

His other concern was the ring. It represented action and he was afraid of it. He knew it had power but instinctively felt he may be unable to control it. He had little use for power and decided that the best place for the ring was at the bottom of the pile of gold. Of Tarnhelm he had much less fear. He had seen that it would allow him to take on any form he wished, but what form did he want? Unable to decide, for a long time, he resisted putting on the helmet for fear of not being able to change back. Eventually he decided to try it on for a few seconds and it was immediately obvious to him what form he should take. Dragons hoard gold.[21] They have no need for its beauty nor its barter value. Dragons are cold blooded and can feel, with great intensity, the warmth of gold's radiance that Fafner craved. Above all, dragons were powerful enough not to heed Fasolt's worrisome trends.

FAFNER

Dragons breathed fire; everyone was afraid of them. What did they care for others? He thought back to the stories he had heard about dragons. There were some stories of dragons that were kind and friendly but Fafner had little time for these; he had his gold to guard. The only threat to dragons seemed to be a certain breed of young men who deemed the defeat of a dragon essential to their own maturity and fame and who came looking for dragons with lances and iron swords. Even with a few minutes experience of a dragon's body Fafner could not see how a dragon would be susceptible to such weapons which, according to legend, seemed to be able to pierce their scales and defy their fiery breath. It seemed impossible, yet the tales were common enough. The dragons that succumbed to these seemingly magical heroes were those who indulged in certain activities that attracted the ire of the human race. Stories of devouring crops and the abduction of young maidens seemed to be the trigger for the activities of these young men. Fafner's slow mind came to the realisation that Fasolt tendencies were to be suppressed even more and might not be wholly lacking, even in dragons. Crop devouring and causing devastation did not interest him. He was too old to take any pleasure in vandalism. There were enough creatures in and around the cave that could fall victim to his breath to keep him from starving. Resigned, Fafner put on Tarnhelm and the shape of a dragon suited him so well that he soon found Tarnhelm unnecessary.

He wrapped his cold body round the warm gold and slept. Time passed and disturbances were rare. During his waking hours, his greatest pleasure was the roasting of swallows of which he became inordinately fond. A few young men who had heard of his hoard came and challenged him but at first sight of his breath and apparently impenetrable scales they had fled. The gold lulled him into a trance-like existence but his Fasolt tendencies and fear of the ring persisted, leaving him feeling tired and old in his bones. Perhaps, one day, it would be time to leave the gold behind.

He is vaguely aware that an old adversary of his, Alberich, has been outside his cave for some time. This does not worry him in the least. No doubt Alberich thinks he will be able to steal the gold somehow and wishes to get his hands on the ring in order to influence events. But Fafner knows there is no physical way that Alberich can steal the gold.

Alberich is merely watching and waiting. He has been waiting a long time. He knows about Siegfried and feels nothing but scorn for his brother's aspirations, being confident of his ability to remove his brother once that fool Siegfried has done his work. One night he is suddenly disturbed from his thoughts by the arrival of the Wanderer, whom he has no difficulty in recognising, despite the night's darkness. Alberich assumes that Wotan is also after the gold. This worries him and he reminds Wotan that he will be unable to obtain or use the gold because of the deals outlined on his spear. He taunts Wotan with his fear that the ring will fall into Alberich's hands and Valhalla be destroyed. Wotan, though, surprises him by the gentleness of his replies. Wotan clearly no longer has any use for the gold, nor the ring and says that fate must play out its hand. As far as Wotan is concerned Alberich may have the gold if he wishes and may do his worst with it. The fate of the gold may be played out in contest between Alberich and his brother. There is Siegfried to be considered, of course, but Siegfried knows nothing of the power of the gold and does not covet it. Alberich is suspicious but Wotan shouts to Fafner that a great hero is coming to kill him and suggests he should give up his gold to Alberich. Fafner recognises Wotan and, realising that he is not a threat, merely replies that he is pleased that his next meal is on its way. Wotan again indicates to Alberich that he may do his worst without any interference from him. These words, which would previously have delighted Alberich, are stated with such authority and resignation that Alberich is not sure that this is still desirable. Wotan leaves Alberich with some tenderness and as Alberich merges into his rocky cleft to continue his watchfulness he feels disturbed and thoughtful.

Wotan too is thoughtful. A little way off he sits down and begins to contemplate deeply. In the process he summons up Erda[22] who appears to us out of the nearby rock, visible from the waist up and shrouded in her customary blue light. Wotan asks for counsel and Erda replies with mystical incantations that sleep is dreaming and her dreaming purpose. Perhaps Wotan should ask the Norns[23], Erda's daughters, who spin the thread of fate. Wotan is unimpressed "They can only spin and observe and can change nothing." He says. "I come to ask you how I can change things." "Why not ask Brünnhilde our daughter?" asks Erda "Because I banished her for rebellion." "You are the teacher of rebellion." Says Erda, "You are not the strong and just person you think you are. Just let me sleep." Wotan is stung by this and says, "Perhaps you are not the all wise dreamer." But Wotan knows Erda is right. He goes on to tell her that he has learnt much. He is resigned to his future and no longer fears the end of his rule. However, he does not want to leave his heritage for Black Alberich to inherit but for his own race of the Volsungs. He tells her that Siegfried will win the ring by his own efforts and without Wotan's help. He hopes that, because Siegfried knows no fear and is not aware of the power of the ring, Alberich's curse will have no effect on him. He hopes that Siegfried and their mutual child Brünnhilde will set the world and his

own spirit free from the dwarf's threat, the curse of the ring and his own compromises. Then perhaps Erda can sleep peacefully. With that, he allows Erda to sleep again but Wotan wonders if he has failed to convince her.
Wotan stays and waits for Siegfried.

At dawn, following Wotan's night-time visit, Fafner was again disturbed by the arrival of more people outside his cave. A short time later he heard a fine blast on a horn and was impressed enough to take a look. He immediately recognised a total lack of fear: such a clean confident young man, such a fine note on the horn, such a strong iron sword with a bright hypnotic glow from the sun's reflection. How good it would be to be rid of the ring, to be reconciled with Fasolt: to be free. The gold would be going home. There was a mild skirmish, but it was a relief for Fafner to offer up his neck to the bright sharp sword.

Chapter 10: Siegfried

It was not only Fafner who was disturbed by the arrival of Siegfried and Mime in the clearing in front of the cave.

Alberich hiding in his cleft in the rocks nearby also observes their arrival. He is puzzled to hear Mime telling Siegfried that this, finally, is where he will learn about fear.
Mime tells Siegfried to avoid the dragon's gaping jaws, his poisonous spittle and his thrashing tail but all Siegfried wants to know is whether the dragon's heart is in the usual place. On hearing this is so, Siegfried blithely pronounces that Nothung will soon pierce it. Mime persists in trying to convince Siegfried that he will soon discover fear and that Siegfried should come to him after the fight. Refusing again to recognise his own fear Siegfried dismisses Mime and drives him away from the clearing.

> "Out of my sight! Leave me alone.
> I'll stay here no longer if you start again about love
> With that nauseating nodding and blinking.

When shall I be free of this dolt!"

Mime slinks off, muttering to himself that it would be best for everyone if the giant and Siegfried would slay each other.

Then Siegfried surprises us. Before turning to the dragon, he sits down under a tree and listens to the birdsong in the forest. He whittles himself a pipe from the nearby reeds and tries to emulate their music.[24]

Mime had no idea what drove Siegfried into the forest day after day. He knew that Siegfried immersed himself in the natural things around him and would frequently play on a pipe or any other instrument he could fashion. As a small child Siegfried would beat out his own rhythms on the anvil or any resonant article, or drum-like instrument that Mime could fashion. Mime had encouraged this. He had given him a horn and had taught Siegfried what little knowledge of music he had; for Mime, in his own way, had loved the child and had brought him up as best he could within the limitations of his own ambitions. But Siegfried had longed for unlimited love, which he instinctively felt was lacking, and had found himself hating Mime for his inability to provide it. In the forest he was closest to his longed for but dimly conceived parents. He would spend hours listening to the music of the forest: wind rustling in the trees, birdsong, the cries of animals, even the growling of the beasts and the many and varied sounds of the rivers and lakes. He could see in these sounds, and in his own attempts to emulate them, something that was always just out of reach. The music provoked a kind of longing which, with his limited experience of life, was his only emotional expression. He had observed the animal life around him: how the mothers would care for their own offspring, feed them and protect them: sometimes at a risk to their own lives. He noted how animals would find a mate and settle down in their nests, holes or lairs together. With his limited understanding of human contact, Siegfried recognised a need for these things in himself and the rhythms of his music were the closest he could get. While he knew only Mime, his visual imagination of his mother, or his mate, was something akin to a roe deer but as music, she was a supreme being. Great rhythmic sounds would dwell in his head as he contemplated on the wonders that existed in the world beyond his knowledge and on the nature of his own mother.

Under the trees with his reed pipe he sings softly to himself of his mother and then notices a bird of a type new to him.

> "But what did my mother look like? I can't imagine.
> Her soft lustrous eyes, surely shone like the roe deer's
> but far more lovely!
> When she bore me in sorrow
> why then did she die?
>
> You pretty bird! I never heard you before:
> do you live in this forest?
> If I understood your sweet song
> you would surely be saying something to me,
> perhaps about my dear mother?
> A testy dwarf once told me
> that one could come to understand bird talk.
> How could that be possible?"

But there is work to do. Considering his foe inside the cave, Siegfried realises that, comforting as it might seem, he cannot be forever dreaming about a mythical mother or female playmate and that success in the real world may require a different attitude. He throws away his puny whistle, draws three mighty blasts from his horn and summons his dragon to battle.

Before he dies, Fafner asks who has killed him. Siegfried admits he doesn't really know who he is and Fafner advises Siegfried to beware of Mime. As Siegfried withdraws his sword from Fafner's heart some of Fafner's blood drops on his hand. It burns his skin and he licks it to find that suddenly the music of the forest is clearer and that he can understand the birds' song! Siegfried's growing maturity has resulted in a further understanding of the natural world. These new birds are messengers from Erda and Siegfried has no difficulty in recognising them as the voices of understanding, reason and common sense. The birds give him advice about the treasure and tell him to choose out Tarnhelm with which he could perform great deeds and the ring, which would allow him to rule the world. Accordingly, Siegfried goes into the cave to look for them.

Outside the cave Alberich and Mime quarrel about how to use the treasure. Unfortunately for them both they appear unable to consider compromise. Alberich claims the ring on the grounds that he gave up love and forged it in the first place and Mime points out that he has brought up Siegfried specifically for the purpose of claiming it. Mime offers Alberich the ring if he can have Tarnhelm. After all, did he not forge it himself. Alberich realises that Mime could steal the ring and refuses. The quarrel is bitter but futile, as Siegfried comes out of the cave holding both items and wondering how either of them could be of any use to him. Before Alberich hides himself he whispers to Mime that he should persuade Siegfried to give him the ring and the helmet: for Alberich is mindful of the curse and knows that, if Mime were to obtain the ring, it would not be long before they were in his own hands. Mime asks Siegfried whether he has discovered fear yet, declaring, once again, his great love. Mime reminds him that, while Siegfried was smelting the sword, he had made a fine broth which Siegfried should now drink. The birds, however, have been singing to Siegfried telling him that Mime is treacherous and Siegfried now finds that he can discern Mime's underlying thoughts and intentions.

> "See, you are tired from your great efforts;
> your body must be burning:
> Refresh yourself with this restoring draught."
> Whines Mime.

What Siegfried actually hears is that Mime hates the Volsungs race and is waiting for Siegfried to choke on the broth. Mime will then remove Siegfried's head with his own sword and take the helmet and ring. As the broth is offered, Nothung makes short work of Mime's head, as predicted by Wanderer. Siegfried is surprised to hear laughter from the surrounding rocks but Alberich makes no attempt to confront him directly. Siegfried places Mime's body on top of the pile in the dark of the cave saying,
> "Lie here in the cavern on the treasure!
> You pursued it with plotting and perseverance
> Now you can be lord of its lustre!
>
> Here's a good guardian to protect you from thieves."

As he places Fafner's body in front of the cave's mouth.[25]

The sun is now high and hot and Siegfried is tired. Relaxing once more he lies under the trees and asks the birds if they can find a more faithful companion for him. Although he hated Mime, he now has no companion at all and he laments that he has no parents nor a brother or sister to relieve his loneliness. The birds tell him there is a possible wife for him nearby. She is lying on a mountaintop, surrounded by fire, which none may walk through except great heroes who are not afraid. Siegfried is immediately filled with an excitement and a desire that he cannot yet define. Jumping up he demands that the birds take him there immediately. The birds, however, are in a playful mood and pretend to have forgotten the way. They lead him round in circles until, just before he loses his temper, they lead him on.

As he rushed through the forest Siegfried reflected on recent events. He felt grown up, now that he was at last free of Mime. He was pleased that he had finally stopped pining for his long dead mother and felt ready to move on to a more mature stage of life. He knew that with his increasing learning and experience he could rely to greater extent on his instincts and on the music he perceived in the world around him. He was sure that he had developed a further understanding of human nature and had been right about Mime's intentions. Only one doubt remained: was he capable of the task ahead? Was he worthy of his father's sword?

Nearing the mountaintop of his ultimate desires, an old man with a deep brimmed hat hiding one eye hails him and asks a few questions about himself. Faced with the lord of the ravens, Siegfried's birds suddenly fly away, never to return and, as their calming influence desert him, Siegfried is, once again, a rather brash and intolerant youth. In no mood for banter, he states roughly and rather rudely

"Show me my way or let me pass."

SIEGFRIED

The Wanderer suggests he should have more respect for the aged but Siegfried says he has had enough of the older generation in the form of Mime, whom he has just killed. He implies that he will do the same again if this old man gets in his way. He makes fun of the Wanderer's hat and, when he notices he has lost an eye, tells him to watch out that he doesn't lose the other one very soon. Wanderer tells him that the missing eye is watching him now and it does not like what it sees. Siegfried asks who the wanderer is and Wanderer describes himself as the guardian of the rock, pointing out the flames that can now be seen in the distance as he speaks.

> "I am the keeper of the mountain and I called up the flames that separate you from the maiden. He who wakes her up, makes an end to my might."

The flames rise up further around the mountain and Siegfried sees the way ahead. He calls the Wanderer an obstinate fool and demands roughly that he gets out of his way. At this, Wotan is angry and, filled with the ancient jealously of the deposed father, bars Siegfried's way with his spear.

> "If you do not fear the flames then fear my spear which has shattered your sword once before."

Siegfried makes an understandable mistake and cries:

> "So I have found my father's enemy!"

Nothung smashes Wotan's spear in a second. Wotan, genuinely shocked, picks up the pieces and sighs sadly and almost fondly,

> "Pass on. I cannot stop you."

Selfishly, driven by a force he does not understand, Siegfried rushes on without a further thought for the generation left behind and plunges headlong through the fire. At the top of the mountain he first sees Grane[26] asleep. Then he sees a pile of armour, which he thinks may be a sleeping man. He uses Nothung to prize away the breastplate and eventually realises that this is a woman. Brünnhilde has changed a great deal during her sleep. Her might and her strength have left her. It is not the air of a fearsome Valkyrie that greets Siegfried but the quiet features of beautiful sleeping woman. Siegfried finds that his heart is racing, that his eyes are dazzled and his limbs are faltering. Fear, he realises, seems to be everything Mime warned him about.

"Whom can I call on to help me?
Mother, mother! Think of me!"
He knows that to wake her he must summon his courage and kiss her.

They both knew when it was time for him to leave. As they emerge from the cave for the last time Brünnhilde tells him that it would not be love between them if she could not let him go forth and perform new deeds. She cries.

"What the Gods taught me I have given you: I am now drained of knowledge and deprived of strength but rich in love."

"Please don't be angry if I remain untutored."
Pleads Siegfried "But I have certainly learnt to always think of Brünnhilde"

"Think of your deeds, think of the vows of mutual trust and love and I will be forever with you."

Siegfried gives Brünnhilde the ring and she gives him her horse Grane, reminding him how Grane used to fly in the heavens to do Wotan's bidding and now, even though he had lost his powers, Grane is still that part of her which obeys her instincts.

Siegfried has clearly learnt something from Brünnhilde for he says he will be acting to Brünnhilde's orders:
"I shall perform deeds of valour through your virtue alone
You select my combats. I am sheltered by your shield
I can no longer count myself alone. I am but Brünnhilde's arm.
Wherever I am we shall both be found. You shall be with me on my deeds and I shall be with you on this rock, for we are one"

Brünnhilde summons up her dwindling powers:
"Before you go, I will cast a spell to protect you from your enemies. No weapon will be able to pierce you.
I have no power left to protect your back but, no matter, for I know you will never be foolish enough to turn your back on your enemy."

Brünnhilde watches him ride down the mountain and disappear into the smoke. He may have learnt much from Brünnhilde but he leaves her mountain still brash in his youthfulness, driven by the call of the music of the country around him and entirely confident that Brünnhilde will always be there: like the mother he never had.
The previous generation have missed their chance. They could have taught him that established

institutions have a reason for their existence, that prevailing morals have their wisdom and that others have rights and feelings, which should not be overridden but they had failed. Like many a youth before him, wisdom is for the old and discovery is for the young. Any attempt to impose order is a crime against life and any restrictions are to be overthrown. Soon he will gain a boat and achieve fame along the river; a youth with talent, strength, charm and protection will quickly achieve his fortune. The music of the Rhine bears him along and time loses its meaning.

Brünnhilde broods guiltily upon her rock:

Why did I not protect my loved one's back? Wotan, hear me, I did not protect the boy's back. Am I not still your wish maiden?[27]

Chapter 11: The Gibichung Family

The Rhine has long lost its mystery. It is now a mere conduit for human commerce and politics and is essential to Hagen's commercial activities. Dealing in illicit substances had brought him great riches but, driven by visions of his overbearing father, his true aims remain elusive.

Ultimate political power was the goal set for Hagen by his father. Hagen had his own parallel aim of gaining the respect of his peers. Although half dwarf, his appearance and size was human but his stocky body shape encompassed the physical strength and tenacity of the dwarfish race. Many men feared him but he had the ability to manipulate his companions with a degree of humour and the occasional surprising application of rough charm. He was hampered by the occasional lapse in his behaviour. At these times his eyes would take on a glassy and disquieting stare and he would appear to be carrying on a conversation with someone whom others could not see. Fortunately for Hagen's ambitions, he was usually alone on such occasions, but there were many who considered him physically dangerous. In recent years he had befriended his half brother and sister, who were the heads of a fading aristocratic family - the Gibichungs. All three were the product of the same mother, Grimhilde. Albrich had come across her as a young widowed beauty who's husband's death had left her bereft. She had agreed to satisfy Alberich's desires in exchange for a substantial sum of gold. Pre-warned of Alberich's denunciation of love she had been prepared for a cold and perhaps degrading experience but had quickly discovered that Albrich had a weakness common to many powerful and brutish males. His desire for control meant that it pleased him to pay for pleasure and attention on an incremental basis. Negotiation and subtle withdrawal allowed her to pile up her own hoard of gold and a close observer might have wondered who was really in control during this liaison. The size of her hoard subsequently enabled her to be sufficiently attractive to the then head of the Gibichung family and father of Gunther and Gutrune.[28] Socially adept, comfortable with riches but somewhat pampered, the Gibichung pair were not well equipped to cope when events went against them. Social climbing was their main occupation and financial support for the arts was their main claim to fame, though they were frequently otherwise engaged during the actual events to which they donated.[29] To those who knew them well, Gunther and Gutrune's social climbing hid personal weaknesses. Gunther was seen to be prepared to sacrifice his moral beliefs in order to advance his social and political standing. Gutrune tended to allow others to make decisions for her and felt that she had little genuine control over her own life. She would routinely agree to actions which she knew in her heart were incorrect. Occasionally, in her wish to change this situation, she would suddenly appear to be even more

THE GIBICHUNGS

vampish and acquisitive than her brother. These inconsistencies were taking their toll of Gutrune and her servants had noted an increasing reluctance to rise in the mornings, prolonged bouts of weeping and sudden swings in mood associated with great variations in her appetite.

Hagen had no time for polite social climbing. He humoured his half siblings to gain the acceptance of the society around them for, despite his acknowledged riches and power, Hagen still felt deprived by his racial origins. He felt sneered at by the very people who were the first to involve him in charitable donations and to request funding of their dubious business deals. He knew his own activities met with disapproval but would be tolerated and ignored as long as he played the necessary games with his neighbours. They little suspected his ultimate aim of gaining absolute political power over them. His other reason for supporting the Gibichungs was the position of their mansion. Its situation on a hill above the river provided a strategic, secure and convenient base for purchase of substances in the east, their packaging and transportation and their eventual sale further west.

In the hall of their mansion overlooking the river, the Gibichungs are plotting: it is time Gunther and Gutrune were both married, to provide the Gibichung family with an heir. Hagen, whose sole object is possession of the ring, knows just the right choices for their future spouses. For Gutrune there is a famous warrior, who just happens to be sailing on the river at this moment. For Gunther there is the semi-mythical Brünnhilde, for is she not rumoured to be descended from the very pinnacle of aristocratic families? Both aims will be difficult to achieve and wooing Brünnhilde may even be physically dangerous. Gutrune allows the others to decide her fate. She wonders if this man may

allow her out of the increasingly tight straitjacket in which she finds herself, within the walls of the Gibichung mansion. It emerges, however, that physical danger has little appeal for Gunther; he has no stomach for the hardships necessary to win Brünnhilde.
Hagen is ready with a plan.

> " No matter." He laughs "With some help from Gutrune's beauty and a 'magic' potion (a combined love potion and amnesic drug should be effective) we may win both spouses."

As Hagen predicts, Siegfried soon arrives by boat, blowing his horn and hollering out his desire to meet the local gentry. The Gibichungs are ready. With great show, Siegfried rides from his boat upon Grane whom he promptly hands over to Hagen's care. Unfortunately, he appears to have forgotten Brünnhilde's explanation of Grane's important position. Siegfried boldly announces that he comes in friendship and has nothing to offer but his strong arm. This remark causes Hagen to remind him of his famed gold and helmet. Siegfried replies that he has no time for trinkets and all he has of the treasure is this strange helmet, attached to his belt. Hagen enlightens him as to the use of the helmet.

> "It is the finest magical work of the Nibelung smiths. Place it on your head and it will transform you into any shape you want and transport you to any place you wish to be."

He carries on to ask about the ring and appears dismayed to hear that it is in the safe hands of a beautiful woman.

Hagen's plans are temporarily foiled, but not so Gutrune's. She is clearly pleased with her prospects. Here at last is someone from outside who may be less dismissive of her position and, what is more, he is a fine, strong, good-looking fellow; not a member of the aristocracy, perhaps, but reputedly rich and seemingly naive enough to be swayed by her charms and moulded into a satisfactory and attentive consort.

And so, the Gibichung family go to work on Siegfried. Great warrior he certainly is but the Rhine aristocracy have no fear of his strong arm and he has no defence against their wiles. Sophisticated seductions, impeccable manners and calculated flattery combine to lull him into a false security. Subtle drugs, and a stunningly refined woman constantly paying court to him serve to complete his complacency. Naively he considers that here, at last, is the recognition he deserves from the sort of company he craves.

How jealous that fool Mime would have been. Look Mime, look Brünnhilde, see how far I have come since I left the forest and the mountain.

Just as he is not fully protected against physical attack so Siegfried has not fully embraced Brünnhilde's wisdom. Brought up in strange circumstances, with poor social skills and thrust precipitously into glamorous society: Siegfried's fall is a familiar story. Inexperienced, overconfident and fresh from his first sexual encounter Siegfried is easy prey for the Gibichungs, as they expose his inner weaknesses which, like his fear, are unrecognised and unacknowledged by himself. Siegfried is slyly introduced to his own inner dark Hagen, his own inner acquisitive Gunther and his own inner fatalistic and ultimately helpless Gutrune. Alas, the hero was already well snared and intoxicated by his own perceived brilliance long before Gutrune struck the last blow by introducing him to Hagen's fatal concoction. He commenced his acquaintance with the Gibichungs by crudely drinking to Brünnhilde but as, the room swam, walls heaved, and colours, perceptions and morals changed, he was soon declaring his undying love for Gutrune and his unswerving loyalty to the Gibichung cause. In his drug-driven confusion he betrays those values he once thought he held strong. The placing of Tarnhelm on his head signifies the extent of his fall. It is Siegfried's own inner Gunther who climbs the mountain for a second time.

For Siegfried has so fallen that he has sworn blood brotherhood to Gunther and, with Brünnhilde forgotten, his eyes blaze upon Gutrune with such desire that she cannot meet his gaze. Gunther tells him that he has no wish to prevent him marrying Gutrune but there is a small task he could perform for Gibichung's cause first. They cut their forearms, let the blood drip into a goblet of wine and drink to their new brotherhood. Both are foolishly amused when Hagen refuses to join in on the grounds that his blood is unsuitable.

A storm is coming and Brünnhilde is disturbed. Her sister, Valtraute, arrives on her horse, from out of the gathering clouds.

"Has Wotan relented?" Is Brünnhilde's first cry. "Will he take me back?"

"No, no I have come against Wotan's command. He is no longer our war-father. He went out into the world as Wanderer and came back with his spear broken. Now he does little except sit in Valhalla, waiting for his ravens to return with the news he expects. No more heroes, no more battles, no more golden apples: he is waiting for the end. He has piled up logs from the world ash tree[30] around Valhalla and is waiting for it to burn. Brünnhilde, he thinks of you often and wishes you would return the ring to the Rhinemaidens, for only that sacrifice will save the Gods and the world from its curse. Only that sacrifice will return the world to its innocent state. That is why I have risked his wrath to come to you."

But wish maiden though she used to be, Brünnhilde refuses to give back the ring. Siegfried entrusted the ring to her in love for safekeeping. Wotan has not relented on her punishment and Brünnhilde knows that, with the ring, and free of Wotan's influence, Siegfried is in a position to unwittingly destroy the Gods. Valtraute has to return in fear and dread back to Valhalla.

Without warning the mountain flames suddenly leap up and Brünnhilde is excited to realise that she will soon see Siegfried once more. Her excitement turns to fear as a stranger arrives who insists on claiming her as his bride. She refuses but he is clearly prepared to use physical violence as he rips the ring off her finger. For a brief moment she seems to see Siegfried through his disguise[31]. Her wisdom, however, is failing and she concludes that slavery to this stranger is Wotan's ultimate punishment, having cruelly teased her with the might of Siegfried. Brünnhilde falls into despair as she is forced into the cave for the night but, as he herds her towards it, Siegfried turns and, to our relief and presumably Brünnhilde's, announces that his sword will lie between them as a symbol of chastity. On taking the form of Gunther, Siegfried has embraced the man's morals but perhaps not yet those of Hagen and his father.

Hagen had sat alone a long time in the huge portal of the Gibichung's mansion watching Siegfried's boat sail off towards the mountain and noting his own and his competitors' freight along the Rhine. Brooding over him in the vast space were three massive marble statues of Wotan, Donner and Fricka. Hagen had good reason to be satisfied as he gloated over the irony of how Siegfried would triumph over the mountain fire and bring back Brünnhilde as captive. Hagen felt sure he would soon have the ring in his own possession. As he gazed over the river, tiredness overtook him and he was unsurprised to see his father appear before him.

"Are you asleep?" Asks Alberich. "Do you hear me? Me, whom rest and sleep betrayed."

Hagen knows his father and what he represents well. Hagen is intent on ultimate personal and political power but he recognises Alberich as the force that drives us towards corruption and ultimately the logic that the destruction of those who oppose us is the necessary course of action. In the past, Hagen had tried to get away from the influence of his father. This time, in despair, he wails that he has had no joy of being born, his mother neglected him in favour of the Gibichungs and his childhood was free from innocence. Above all, he is unable to be happy. But his father is ready.

"Hate the happy." He growls. " Love only your father and we shall inherit the earth from the Gods. Beware of Siegfried for my curse cannot harm him. He is free from knowledge of evil and ambition. Swear to be true to me my son."

Alberich is clearly not all knowing and Hagen will only swear to be true to himself. He knows that Siegfried is no longer to be feared, for has not Siegfried already succumbed to those false attractions dangled before him by the Gibichung family?

Hagen wakes to a beautiful dawn: the river is dazzling in the sun and the mountains peaks thrust their way through the mists. Clearly a day when his longed for happiness may be within his grasp. True to Hagen's own thoughts Siegfried arrives, apparently using Tarnhelm to transport him back. Siegfried has learnt much in the short time he has been with the Gibichungs. Gutrune runs in full of happiness and Siegfried gaily announces that he has won her as a wife by capturing Brünnhilde. He tells how he brought Brünnhilde down the mountain, and switched with Gunther. Now Gunther and Brünnhilde are sailing home in Siegfried's boat and will soon arrive. Siegfried and Gutrune run off joyously to make preparation for their wedding.

Hagen, who is not without a sense of humour, nor insensitive to the happiness of the couple, rings out the alarm bells summoning the local populace to the mansion. They soon come, armed and expecting some sort of conflict. They are amused to find that they have been tricked by Hagen and will be attending a double wedding feast, instead of the expected battle. Hagen's wit is much admired by the happy crowd as they gather to watch Gunther and Brünnhilde disembark from Siegfried's boat. Gunther is full of pride and welcomes the crowd with a little speech of thanks and joy for the forthcoming weddings but the crowd cannot help noticing that his bride-to-be seems to be in a different mood. Brünnhilde keeps her head down during these proceedings, taking little interest in her surroundings, until the moment when Gunther mentions the names of those who are to be wed. At the mention of Siegfried she looks up to see him standing close by. To her amazement Siegfried calmly introduces himself and Gutrune.

"Siegfried does not know me!" She cries and nearly faints. As she stumbles, Siegfried catches her and she notices the ring on his finger. Even as she demands to know how the ring got there, she realises that it was not Gunther who braved the flames but Siegfried. Gunther is now in despair that his cowardice is exposed to Brünnhilde and his hard earned reputation could soon be destroyed.

Siegfried too is bewildered.
"I won that ring killing a dragon." He states, "Not from any woman." The effects of Hagen's drugs, Siegfried's selective amnesia and maybe his self-deception are clearly continuing and already Siegfried has apparently forgotten the events of last night. Perhaps, at Gutrune's suggestion, he has already helped himself to some concoction during his short time alone with her.

Happily for Gunther's political aspirations the crowd seem uninterested in explanations, but Hagen seizes his chance.
"Do you know this ring?" he asks Brünnhilde. Brünnhilde states that Siegfried gave her the ring as her own husband, that Gunther stole it from her and now the ring was on Siegfried's finger. "What does this say about Gunther's honour?" She asks. Siegfried remains bewildered and says it is all nonsense but suddenly he impulsively mentions the drawn sword that lay between them last night in the cave. Here is a clear breach in Siegfried's story and further confirmation to Brünnhilde that it was not Gunther who braved the fire on the second occasion.

Brünnhilde is consumed with vengeance and dismay and lies that the sword remained in its sheath and that she is Siegfried's rightful bride.
Hagen again seizes the initiative.

" Here is my spear" he shouts "You will each swear that your story is true and if either of you prove false then by this spear shall you fall."

Siegfried seizes the blade and swears that if he has been false to his blood brother and should Brünnhilde's story prove true, then the spear shall pierce him to the death. At this Brünnhilde grabs the shaft declaring that Siegfried shall perish by its point for his false oath.

Gunther and Gutrune have little idea what Hagen is up to and Siegfried prefers to find the whole thing a joke. Laughingly he suggests to Gunther that Brünnhilde is tired and should rest before the wedding and remarks that mere males have little knowledge of female passions and waywardness. The crowd fall in with Siegfried and bear him off, arm in arm with Gutrune, for more celebrations. They leave Gunther, Brünnhilde and Hagen to decide their next action.

Faced with such trickery by Siegfried, Brünnhilde's God-like status, her wisdom and her instincts have all abandoned her. Feeling that evil must be fought with evil she naturally turns to Hagen for help. "Who is there that can avenge me on Siegfried?" She asks. Hagen gallantly offers his honour. Honour and success in battle against Siegfried seem so remote from Hagen's abilities that Brünnhilde can only be scornful about his chances. "A glance from his eye in battle will be enough to defeat you." She says. Hagen reminds her of Siegfried's oath on his spear point and asks if she has any counsel for him. " Indeed." says Brünnhilde.

"My spells have rendered that part of him which he presents to the world invulnerable but his back is not protected."
"There shall my spear strike."   Shouts Hagen in triumph.

Hagen now feels he has within his power all those aspects of our lives that he needs in order to obtain effective possession of the ring: Siegfried's brightness, Brünnhilde's wisdom and intuition, the public face of Gunther and the sterile emotion of Gutrune are all now in his sway. He points out to Gunther that Siegfried endangers his position and reputation, should his memory improve. Brünnhilde assists Hagen by mocking Gunther's cowardice in sending Siegfried to win a bride for him.

   "What can be done?" Asks Gunther
   "We must kill Siegfried." Says Hagen, simply.

But Gunther is shocked at this suggestion for he is not altogether evil himself, nor is he a murderer. He reminds Hagen about his blood brotherhood arrangement with Siegfried. Hagen, points to Brünnhilde and suggests this may have already been broken by Siegfried. He finalises his argument by reminding Gunther about Siegfried's ring and treasure and suggests that, as Siegfried's brother in law, this would become Gunther's property, making him as rich as he desires. Brünnhilde agrees enthusiastically with all this, as only the death of Siegfried will suffice for the position in which his betrayal has placed her. Gunther has some lingering qualms and asks about Gutrune.

"How can we face her with Siegfried's blood on our hands?"

THE GIBICHUNGS

Here Brünnhilde appears to gain some insight but, in her jealousy, assumes the wrong enemy. Clearly the other woman is responsible for all this. She has used the magic, nay the witchcraft, of her beauty to seduce and confuse Siegfried. It is right that she should suffer.

Hagen suggests that a hunting accident can be arranged for Siegfried so that Gutrune will not blame them. So do all three agree on a gruesome path to secure the end of Siegfried, each for their own different reasons. Suddenly there are sounds of rejoicing. Siegfried and Gutrune are borne aloft in front of the merry crowd taking them towards their wedding vows. The three plotters draw apart and join the procession, their eyes fixed on the happy couple who are to be the real prey in the morrow's hunt.

Next day Siegfried has no success at the hunt. Convinced he is now following a wood sprite rather than a bear, he becomes separated from the rest of the party and finds himself climbing down towards a rarely frequented bank of the Rhine. Here the river has many of the features of our first acquaintance. Well protected from sight by surrounding cliffs and with dense trees to produce shade, it is cool and dark. Shrouded in swirling mist with bog plants covering the river's edge: it is not obvious where the water begins and the land ends. Waiting for Siegfried are the three Rhinemaidens. They are in a surprisingly happy mood, for they have heard of a recent prophecy by the three Norns, who spin fate's rope. The prophecy states that "Dame Sun" will send them a hero whose demise will give them back their gold. Convinced that the time is soon coming when the gold shall be theirs once more they are unable, by their very nature, to resist a flirtation with the great hero Siegfried. Hearing his horn they dive into the deep. Siegfried arrives seconds later with a great curse that he has lost his prey.

" Siegfried" They sing to him from the waters edge, "Why are you complaining?"

"Ha! Have you lured away my prey? But perhaps he is your lover? If so I will happily leave him to you."

"What will you give us in return for your prey?"

"I have caught nothing else all day so you can name your price."

"That ring on your finger perhaps."

"No, not that. I slew a great dragon for that ring. I'll not give that away for a bearskin. My wife would scold me if I did."

"Does she beat you Siegfried? Only married one day and already he feels the weight of her hand."

"So handsome." Sings one Rhinemaiden
"So strong." Sings another
"So desirable." Sings the third
"And so mean." taunt all three, laughing as they again dive deep into the water.

"How can I stand such mockery?" Laughs Siegfried. "Come on then you three you may have the ring."

The Rhinemaidens return but are now rather more serious. They tell Siegfried about the prophecy.

"Keep the ring Siegfried. He who made it and lost it in shame placed a curse on it that anyone who wears it is doomed to die as a result. As you slew the dragon so shall you be slain this very day. This is foretold in the twists of the Norns rope. Only the waters of the Rhine can wash the ring clean."

"Ha! I was wary of your flirting but your threats frighten me less. This sword shattered a spear and will split the rope. Know that, if all the ring could do is to provide worldly wealth, I would not value it and, if you were to give me genuine love in exchange, you would have it. But you will not get it by threats."
Siegfried throws a sod of earth over his shoulder and continues. "As for my life and limb I value them thus."

The Rhinemaidens swim away singing,
"We tell you secrets you are too stubborn to heed. A proud woman will inherit your treasure and she will understand us."

They leave Siegfried knowing that he had learnt something more of the ways of women and feeling rather resentful that, but for his commitment to Gutrune and the ring, he might have done well to choose one of those beautiful swimming women for himself.
Perhaps Siegfried was right not give the ring to the Rhinemaidens. It is never a good course to give in to the song of the siren. But things will surely continue to go hard with Siegfried while his stubbornness prevails and he continues to deny his fear and forget about Brünnhilde.

The mists are clearing and Siegfried is reluctantly pulled back from his dreams of mermaids, to harsher reality, by the sound of a Gibichung horn and Hagen shouting his name. He puts his own horn to his lips and calls the hunting party down to the cool shade by the river. Gunther, Hagen and the attending colourful company and vassals soon descend the cliff. Wine, skins, fruit, good cheer and roasting meat are all soon laid out as a feast is prepared before the company moves on to the next kill.

Siegfried has to bear some good-natured chaffing about his lack of hunting success and he counters by recounting that he might have caught three fine water birds, who told him that he would be slain on this very day. At this Gunther appears morose but Hagen remains calm and hands Siegfried a drinking horn as he prepares to bait the trap.

"It is said that you can hear bird song Siegfried"

"I have not heeded their chirping for a long time. Gunther! My blood brother, be cheerful. Here drink from the same horn as myself."

But Gunther is depressed and seems to want to warn Siegfried.

"The horn has your blood in it." He says. "It is insipid and pale."

"Then I shall mix it with yours." Says Siegfried and pours Gunther's drink into his.

Quietly to Hagen, Siegfried asks if Brünnhilde is still causing Gunther concern.

"It is a pity he cannot understand Brünnhilde as well as you hear birdsong." Replies Hagen.

"Ha! Since I heard women's voices I have not bothered with birds, nor the things of the forest!" Boasts Siegfried, looking round at the forest and perhaps beginning to remember his origins.

"But once you did understand birdsong?" Persists Hagen

"Yes!" shouts Siegfried, who jumps to his feet impulsively. "Gunther, would you like to hear a song of my boyhood?"

"Very much" replies Gunther, who has no idea of Hagen's purpose. The crowd agree with Gunther and all sit down to hear Siegfried's tale.

So Siegfried starts to sing. As he does so he brings forth music from the forest. Once again, the trees rustle to his tune and rivers peal to his rhythm. Birds accompany his story and even the cries of beasts punctuate the drama. The watchers are drawn in, enchanted and engrossed. They hear Mime's endless whining as Siegfried sings of his upbringing by the scheming dwarf, whose only plan for him was to kill the dragon and then to kill him. They feel Siegfried's longing for his mother, as for their own. They hear the rhythm of the anvil as Siegfried reforges Nothung. They tremble at the voice of Fafner, as Siegfried moves in for the kill. They are enchanted as Siegfried bids them take note of how he could understand the birds after tasting the dragon's blood. They are excited as the birds inform Siegfried of the treasure and of how Tarnhelm and the ring might serve him. His audience are not surprised to find that, under Siegfried's influence, the tales told by the birds around them are now closer to their own understanding and they are near to weeping that they cannot unravel the forest's meaning.

"The ring" shouts Hagen. "Did you take it away?"

"The birds." Shout the others "Did you hear them again?"

"Indeed" says Siegfried. "The ring and Tarnhelm, I gathered up and I listened while the birds told me that Mime intended to poison me with his broth."

"Was this good counsel?" asks Hagen

"Did you repay Mime?" ask the others

"The fool Mime came at me with his broth but I could hear him stammering and muttering about how he was going to kill me and so this very sword laid him low."

"Ha!" shouts Hagen "What he could not forge himself he could still feel."

"What more did the bird say?" Ask the others and momentarily Siegfried looks as if he may have forgotten.

"First drink." Says Hagen, softly. "I have spiced the horn well for you, it will waken your memory so that the past will not slip your mind."

Siegfried drinks Hagen's broth, which is as potent as Mime's and Hagen's trap has sprung.

Siegfried, puzzled, looks for a long time into the drinking horn and then starts to sing again. This time he sings with great gentleness but with a similar mesmerising effect on his audience.

"The birds told me of a wonderful wife, whom I might win for myself. One who was set on a rocky height, surrounded by fire. Whoever could break through the fire- Brünnhilde would be his. Gladly, I followed the birds until I reached the fiery rock. I

THE GIBICHUNGS

> made my way through the flames and there found my reward."

Siegfried is now in full voice. He is carried away by passion and longing and the forest is in full orchestra. His audience share his intense emotions as once again Siegfried is united with Brünnhilde.

> "There I found her in shining armour. I loosened her helmet and my bold kisses awakened her. How ardent was my love for her as I fell into her arms"

Gunther, finally realising the true situation stands up and shouts, "What do I hear?" Siegfried's spell over the company is suddenly broken and he stands in the centre of the company, appearing confused. Two ravens fly from a nearby bush to inform Wotan that the end has come and Hagen moves in for the kill.
Pointing to the circling ravens he says, "Perhaps you can hear their song, Siegfried."
Siegfried turns to look and, before Gunther can stop him, Hagen plunges his spear into Siegfried's exposed back.

As he feels the steel slip through his ribs and pierce his lungs and, as the blood froths up into his throat, Siegfried realises that he had not gained the wisdom he longed for.
Some of the company run to restrain Hagen but are too late.

> "Why?" They ask

> "I have merely avenged perjury." states Hagen.

Realising that it would be impossible to remove the ring at that moment he walks slowly away up the cliff and disappears into the gathering night.

Siegfried opens his eyes and, for a brief moment, there is once again music in the forest.

> "Brünnhilde open your eyes.
> Your awakener came and you laughed in delight.
> The blissful stirring of her breath.
> Blessed fear.
> Brünnhilde bids me welcome."

And he is gone.

After they have recovered from the shock, under the command of the equally shocked Gunther, the vassals make an impromptu funeral carriage from the hunting apparel and light torches from the fire, to see Siegfried home. Siegfried's magic is not yet spent and the music of the forest is not subdued. A funeral march emanates from the trees as Siegfried is raised onto strong shoulders and is borne in state back to the Gibichung mansion. Somewhere along the way, the company's mood alters, the forest music changes key, and for the last few leagues the bearers and vassals feel they are taking part, not in a funeral procession, but in a torch lit triumphal march: as they carry back their hero to be finally united with his true wife.

Back at the mansion Gutrune hears Brünnhilde suddenly laughing in triumph and is filled with foreboding that something terrible has happened. She enters Brünnhilde's bedroom to seek reassurance and finds the room empty. From the window she sees Brünnhilde standing at the river edge where she is in counsel with the Rhinemaidens. In the distance, Gutrune sees the torches of the procession but, not hearing Siegfried's horn, she knows something has gone terribly wrong. Rushing down towards the river herself she meets Hagen, who is the first to arrive. He

THE GIBICHUNGS

shouts to Gutrune that her pallid husband returns and that a wild boar has put an end to his hunting. The vassals lay Siegfried down by the Rhine. Gutrune throws herself at the body and realises that this was not a boar. Distraught, she accuses her brother of being the murderer but he tells her that Hagen was the accursed boar. Hagen calmly justifies himself on the grounds of the oath Siegfried swore on his spear and now he claims the ring on the grounds of a sacred right of reparation. Gunther however begs to differ and claims the ring as his property as brother-in law. Immediately they fight and, before the crowd can part them, Gunther lies dead, struck by Hagen's spear even before his own sword is out of its scabbard. Triumphant, Hagen reaches for the ring, confident that he has finally removed all obstacles to his progress towards ultimate rule.

But in death, Siegfried has been united with Brünnhilde who is standing quietly behind his body. Observing Gutrune's genuine dismay and the results of Gunther's and Hagen's greed, has finally reunited Brünnhilde with her wisdom and instinct and it is clear to her now what has happened and what needs to be done. The combined magic of Siegfried and Brünnhilde is too powerful for Hagen for, as he reaches towards the ring, Siegfried's arm rises up pulling away from Hagen and towards Brünnhilde. Brünnhilde easily slips the ring off his finger and claims her true inheritance.

Gutrune shouts at Brünnhilde that her jealousy has brought about the whole disaster but Brünnhilde gently tells her that Gutrune was never Siegfried's wife only a paramour and that Siegfried had always belonged to herself. Gutrune than turns on Hagen and the crowd are amazed to learn of the potion which caused Siegfried to lose his memory. Brünnhilde, however, is no longer surprised at this and is already preparing for her own and Siegfried's final triumph. She orders a great pile of wood to be set up around Siegfried's body at the Rhine's edge and, takes up a flaming torch. Mounting Grane, she starts to sing with remarkable power. The effect on the assembled company easily equates to Siegfried's performance in the forest earlier in the day.

> "No man more honest ever took an oath. No man more pure in love was so betrayed. He, who deceived me, was loyal to his friend Gunther for he did separate himself from me with his sword."

She points heavenwards.

> "You the heavenly custodian of oaths. Feel your guilt, for you sacrificed him. This innocent had to betray me so that I could become wise again. I know your will. Everything is clear to me. He and I are one. Rest now you Gods, for our sacrifice will redeem you."

She points to the people around her.

> "You and I are one.[32] The sufferings of each is the sufferings of all. He who does you wrong does himself wrong and he who does you injury, injures us all. Compassion shown by one is compassion by us all. Sacrifice by one shall redeem you all and, by this sacrifice, will Brünnhilde and Siegfried release you from your longing. Gone will be your unjust laws, your corrupt politics, your fickle Gods, money, judges, infirmities and idols. Only self respect and love shall remain. My eyes were opened by the profoundest suffering of grieving love. I saw the world's end and all shall surely reach the great oneness of being!

THE GIBICHUNGS

I take up the ring and give it away to the daughters of the Rhine. They shall take the ring from my ashes. The fire and the waters of the Rhine shall wash away the curse.
Fly away you ravens, back to Wotan, pass by Brünnhilde's rock and direct Loge to Valhalla for the end of the Gods is nigh and I throw this torch at Valhalla's vaults."

At this Brünnhilde throws the torch on the huge pile of wood that has been built up around Siegfried's body and, at the slightest nudge from Brünnhilde's heel, Grane leaps into the flames.

" Siegfried, Siegfried your wife joyfully greets you."

According to many witnesses the result was immediate and spectacular. The flames leapt skyward as far as Valhalla which, in truth, had never been very far away. The riverbank was consumed in flame and the Rhineland for miles around was lit in its magnificent glow. Then they saw the river swelling, just as it did for Alberich, but this time its banks were breached and a deep flood became inevitable. The people rushed for the hills and turned to see the flames quenched by the flood. All wondered at the magnificent sight of the three Rhinemaidens swimming towards the remains of the fire with the Rhine lit up by the flames of Valhalla[33] burning fiercely overhead. Hagen who had been increasingly distraught over the behaviour of Brünnhilde could stand it no longer. He rushed into the flood, shouting at the Rhinemaidens to keep away from the ring. He was immediately embraced by the treacherous mermaids and carried down into oblivion, so the seed of the Nibelung became reunited once again with the mud of the Rhine. The Rhinemaidens were last seen swimming gaily back into the main channel of the river, carrying the ring aloft.

Epilogue: Wotan

It didn't work, of course. Wotan hadn't expected it to: he had never been impressed by the 'oneness of being' theory.

Great things had certainly happened. The Rhine had flooded and had found a new course.[34] The sea had broken through into the far Western swamps, producing a new island. Above all, the disruption had finally caused them to create their new monotheistic God[35], which Wotan could see was already corrupted.

We find Wotan (a much wiser and more complete being than when we first met him) contemplating on what he had learnt. He was sitting amongst the ruins of Valhalla in a thoughtful and allegorical mood. One major realisation was that the loss of his eye in order that he might see within himself, did not mean the immediate gaining of wisdom. It was merely the beginning of the journey.

Right from the beginning he had seen this new requirement coming. Refusing to acknowledge it he had fought it and created offspring to help him. He had made many errors. The ring hadn't helped him, not with Alberich still loose. The fortress of Valhalla was a mad joke. Siegmund and Sieglinde had been good fun as wolves but the idea had been misguided. Eventually he had accepted that he needed to re-create himself in the required new image by incorporating the qualities of the other Gods and demi-Gods, as necessary. But this had caused unforeseen effects and now to rule without love or passion could no longer be his aim. By the time Siegfried had arrived, events had taken their own course. He was glad the spear had been broken.

The talk with Alberich had been the turning point. The dialogues with Mime and Alberich, undertaken with concern and without the usual rancour, made the final incorporation of Black Alberich possible. He knew he could cope with this, for Alberich was offset by a love of beauty and of life and companionship which Wotan had learnt from Freya. Also necessary, was the appreciation of devotion, duty and bravery that he finally learnt saying goodbye to his beloved Brünnhilde on that awful night on the mountain. He had almost given up altogether, until her love for him broke his depression and despair. He knew that these qualities were more than a balance for the less attractive aspects of Alberich. Surprisingly Alberich had proved to have some good points. There was a useful appreciation of life and beauty. This was different from Freya's and mixed with a deep longing that Wotan found painful to live with but which he recognised as a spur to achieve. Any tendency towards temper or violence he was finding increasingly easy to suppress. He never liked Donner much anyway. Loge and he had never been very separate and Wotan grinned. A sense of mischief was, he knew, part of the truly rounded person that is the true gold and rightful ring of our dreams. Froh, he had nearly ignored and what a mistake that would have been. He had recalled that Froh had saved him from his biggest potential mistake when his shout had shocked him into taking Erda's advice and throwing away the ring. Wotan shuddered at the thought of the consequences had he retained the ring. An all-powerful God with a ring cursed and coveted by Alberich was a situation of catastrophic potential. Alberich would have taken over for sure. Wotan had recalled that Froh had intervened on other occasions with similar wisdom and he had embraced Froh to see from whence this ability came. He was surprised to discover a sense of humour, an ability to not take himself too seriously and a tendency to take a wider and more general view. Froh was quiet but effective and, for all Loge's trickery, Wotan was now convinced that Froh was the wiser. His only regret was that he had not recognised these qualities within himself earlier.

No, he no longer wished to take responsibility for their acts. Compromise and deals were not going to go away. There was no going back, like some of them wanted, to a world where inequality and politics did not exist. There never was such a place anyway. A few of them seemed to have the right idea: break down tribal barriers; treat others as you would have them treat you. But their new God was flawed. Deals would soon be required; compromises made and excuses found. The new God would soon have a spear or similar as a burden and a dissatisfaction. Wotan thought it unlikely that even a monotheistic God could avoid, once again, sending an offspring as a solution, and witnessing or causing his or her eventual futile sacrifice. The whole cycle would start again. He hoped that no God of the future would feel the need to sacrifice an offspring. Could such a plan ever work? Perhaps a total innocent was the way: a holy fool who learns compassion through adversity and can teach by example?[36] Wotan sighed - compassion and learning had not been Siegfried's strong points.

He knew why. He knew where they had got it wrong. Their new God wasn't monotheistic at all. He was incomplete. They had left out Alberich!

They were unable to accept a God, or their own psyche, with a dark side so they had created a separate Alberich-figure who will continue to steal their gold. They had even given him horns and a tail, and a fiddle to play. Wotan gave a wry smile; Alberich would have loved that. So they will have: sin with sex, power with religion, self-aggrandizement with politics, hate with race and they will continue to blame Black Alberich, instead of looking for him within.

As for himself, a life of contemplation, quietness and study beckoned. He would try to help where he could and distribute wisdom where possible. There was still one remaining problem, however. He rose heavily, and began to search amongst the ruins of Valhalla: amongst the barriers he had set up to protect himself from his own completeness. Fricka was there somewhere and he had some explaining to do.

Appendix 1. Sources

My own sources are Wagner's music and libretti and the bibliography below. Wagner's sources were Norse mythology and Germanic medieval heroic stories. Much of the Norse mythology has been lost. The Teutonic tribes who originated these tales were of Euro-Asian origin. They probably brought with them early Asian mythology. Within Europe they tended to divide up into three broad groups. The Goths, who migrated southwards and came under Greek and Roman influence, the Anglo-Saxon and German tribes, occupying central Western Europe and, later, England and the Norsemen who occupied Scandinavia. Although there are a number of Germanic poems and sagas, it is the northern tribes that we mostly have to thank for retaining their myths in written form, probably because Paganism hung on in these inaccessible areas until the tenth century. Even so, the main sources were written late enough to come under Christian influences. The old beliefs continued to hang on a lot longer. Saxo Grammaticus, writing around 1200 and, judging by his writings, no mean scholar wrote, "That the country of Denmark was once cultivated and worked by giants, is attested by the enormous stones attached to the barrows and caves of the ancients."

Many of the Northern sagas were gathered together in two collections called the 'Eddas'. The oldest of these, the Elder or poetic edda was written around 1200 and discovered in a farmhouse in Iceland in the 17th century. The other known as Prose Edda was written in the 13th century by Snorri Sturluson, who recorded many old myths with great accuracy and clear enjoyment of the tales. Saxo Grammaticus, a Danish ecclesiastical historian, although clearly not approving of such idolatry, recorded a number of sagas and histories in pedantic Latin. Wagner's medieval sources included the Nibelungenlied and the Volsung sagas. These are more in the way of chivalrous tales than religious mythology, especially the former, though they, no doubt, drew heavily on the continuing oral tradition.

Appendix 2. The Ring Cycle

This appendix is designed for newcomers to the Ring Cycle, who may be tempted to take things further.

There are good videos of the operas notably by the metropolitan Opera conducted by Levine and the Barenboim version with Anne Evans and John Tomlinson. As with all opera, there is no substitute for the real thing. A traditional production is probably the best starting point for most people.

It's long – at least 16 hours. There are four operas in Wagner's 'Ring of the Nibelung' cycle: Rhinegold, The Valkyrie, Siegfried and Götterdämerung - usually translated as 'Twilight of the Gods'. Rhinegold is a short introduction, being only the length of an average opera. The others are five-hour marathons. Those who are considering attending the Bayreuth festival need to be very patient (at the time of writing, about 8 years) or be members of a Wagnerian society. Black-market tickets may be available for the very rich but, if discovered, the ticket holder may be refused entry and banned thereafter.

Wagner wrote the libretto long before he wrote the music. The libretto of Götterdämmerung was written first and he then worked backwards. After writing each opera he felt compelled to write a further opera explaining the events which had occurred 'previously'. Each new opera involved some rewriting of the other libretti but there are a number of episodes left over in which the action of the previous operas are recounted.

The music was written later in the 'correct' order. Altogether this took twenty-five years.

The music for Götterdämmerung, was finished in 1874. There were earlier performances in Munich, but Wagner first produced the entire Ring Cycle in his specially built theatre in Bayreuth in 1876. The long-suffering Ludwig 11 of Bavaria put up the money, both for his theatre and for the first Ring Festival. The theatre was designed under Wagner's direction specifically for his concept of the Gesamtkunstwerk ('total art work'- an alliance of music, poetry, the visual arts, dance etc). The first festival was beset by technical difficulties and was a financial disaster but was nevertheless generally regarded an artistic triumph. One technical hitch led to the belief that it was Wagner who first introduced the darkened auditorium. At that time it was usual to leave the lights on so that the audience could read the libretto. Wagner wanted the gaslights dimmed, but at the first performance of Rhinegold, the lights in the auditorium went out altogether. This allowed the audience to enjoy the long E flat major, birth of consciousness, start to Rhinegold in darkness, as is usual now.

Apart from its length, the music had at least two other revolutionary features, for the opera of its day. Arias were replaced by themes or leitmotivs, which allude to characters, concepts or objects. They change, develop and fuse as the ideas within the opera develop. They are not merely labels and can carry the action, sometimes informing the listener of connections of ideas or the thoughts of those on the stage.
Bernard Shaw mentions about 20 main themes stating that they are as easy to recognise as a soldier might recognise various trumpet calls. Newman mentions nearly 200 and there are extensive modern classifications by Derek Cooke and Barry Millington.

The number of recognised motifs is probably still rising. Although an admirer of Wagner, Shaw apparently failed to appreciate the true complexity of the music, stating that the average "English amateur singer" could take on the roles of Wotan, Brünnhilde and Siegfried! To be fair to Shaw, he was writing long before there were any decent recording mechanisms and his experience of the Ring was limited to live performances. The other revolution in the music was Wagner's method of achieving resolution between the musical themes particularly by the frequent use of the diminished seventh chord. This was a becoming a common and increasing method of writing in the romantic period. Liszt, from whose music Wagner seems to have learnt the technique, commonly used it. Wagner first introduced it into opera, with devastating effect, in Tristan and Isolde: leading the way towards atonality in opera. Following Tristan he was ready to apply the same technique to the Ring: producing music which seems to flow seamlessly from one dramatic event to the next. These two features of the music enabled the libretti of his operas to become conversational in form, rather than to be written in poetic- style stanzas. Although this form of Wagner's music first appeared to the public in Tristan & Isolde in 1859, Wagner was writing conversational- style libretti for Siegfried's Death (as Götterdämmerung was first called) as early as 1848, long before he had written the music. (The actual form of stanza writing he used at that time was Stabriem). His contemporaries who saw the libretto thought that he had written recitative only. Presumably, even at this early stage, he had a revolutionary form of music in mind.

Appendix 3. Philosophy

Not being an intense student of philosophy, I am indebted to Magee for the following account. I hope I have done him justice.

During the 25 years it took to write the ring it is not surprising that Wagner and his views changed.
In simplistic terms: Wagner wrote the libretto as a revolutionary, influenced by anarchism and also the philosophy of Ludwig Feuerbach, with Siegfried seen as the epitome of revolutionary youth. Most of the music, however, was written under the influence of the philosophy of Schopenhauer. The extent of Wagner's study of Schopenhauer and his knowledge of Schopenhauer's arguments were remarkable.

At the age of 36, under the influence of his friend, anarchist Michael Bakunin, Wagner took part in the failed Dresden uprising of 1849 and was lucky to escape subsequent arrest by fleeing to Switzerland. Bakunin was caught, sentenced to death, reprieved and spent many years in prison. Starting from a desire to create a revolution in the arts Wagner had moved rapidly on to a radical political viewpoint. He was criticised at the time for supporting revolution merely to allow his own art to flourish and, in later life, claimed he had never been an activist. His writings before Dresden, particularly as editor of the communist broadsheet 'Volkblatte' and his activities in Dresden belie this. His attitude to his audience was always ambivalent. He recognised that he needed his upper middle class supporters, yet professed to hate their politics. Hence his stated artistic desire to burn down the opera house plus audience at the end of a performance.

Anarchists at this time were not necessarily violent. Their requirements were to do away with money, marriage and most institutions. Their creed was 'to each according to requirements and from each according to ability'. The underlying fundamental was probably a revolt against the increasing industrialisation of the time. Engels and Marx were part of this political ferment but Marx later scorned the type of views held by Wagner as 'utopian socialism'.

Feuerbach was a member of a group of writers who attracted the appellation 'The young Hegelians'. He wrote that, as a way of coping with uncertainty and fate, it is a basic human need to create Gods in our own image. In a multi-deity system the Gods take on the many sides of our natures and act accordingly. As society becomes more sophisticated the Gods tend to merge. At around the time of his flight to Switzerland, Wagner made an extensive study of Feuerbach. Two points made by Feuerbach are central to Wagner. Firstly, Feuerbach argued that, as society accepted the true nature of religion, a certain maturity of thought would result. This would allow a system in which people would accept greater responsibility for their own lives, instead of relying on a God (or, perhaps God-like individuals). This was essentially an optimistic outlook and fitted well with Wagner's socialism of the time. Later, under Schopenhauer's influence, he was to abandon this view. The other aspect of Feuerbach, which had a profound effect on Wagner's art, was that many religions have a central theme of a God coming to earth and taking upon himself the sufferings of mankind. As we project ourselves onto our Gods, we are saying that to die for the sake of others is the highest moral activity. This theme of redemption was fully explored in Parsival. Wagner appears to have hung on to his belief in the supremacy of the act of redemption during his Schopenhauer years. It was certainly a fruitful theme for his art. Feuerbach also had an influence on George Elliot, who made efforts to ensure that he became better known in the English-speaking world. The pre-eminence of German philosophy at the time is mentioned in 'Middlemarch'.

Schopenhauer's philosophy was based on that of Kant. Despite the logical nature of his views, Kant, in the fashion of his day, utilised some rather obscure phraseology. Schopenhauer was an excellent writer and clarified Kant in more direct language. Schopenhauer then proceeded to muddy the waters with some closely argued metaphysics. Kant put forward the entirely logic view that there are things which we can identify through our senses or recording machines and things which are totally beyond our ken, about which we can know nothing. All sorts of things may exist with which we can make no contact. The world we know is merely a result of our experience and senses and these are limited and fallible. Kant implied that there might be, in existence, a massive reality of which we are totally unaware. He also said that there was no point in speculating on the nature of those things of which we can know nothing. Schopenhauer set about to carry out just that speculation. He concluded that the knowable world was differentiated and the unknown is a single, undifferentiated, spaceless, non-material and inaccessible reality. From this, by close and logical argument, he was led into a number of conclusions. In ethics, his opinion that we are all of us effectively one item led to the views I have distilled within my version of Brünnhilde's speech. The ultimate oneness of being argument has echoes within Hinduism (Brahman) and Buddhism as well as some aspects of Christianity: all of which Schopenhauer and Wagner subsequently studied. Schopenhauer was also led to the pessimistic view that nothing is likely to improve and that the knowable world was a violent and extremely unpleasant place. Accordingly, there is no point in longing for anything at all. The logical conclusion is that withdrawal and a monastic existence is the ultimate way of coping with this situation. His views on religion had much in common with Feuerbach's. He recognised the need for religion but pointed out that the associated stories are metaphorical and exist to assuage our need for reassurance. They may contain profound truths but to take the religious stories as literal truth is fanciful and childish. He expressed the belief that sex and art - particularly music, due to its abstract nature, were the best means to help us to get nearest to the state of mental withdrawal that he saw as the ultimate aim. Wagner took this view to heart and Magee suggests he started to write Schopenhauer-inspired music with the intention of producing music that gets us close to the unknown. The idea of the vital importance of the combination of music and sexual love reaches its zenith in Tristan and Isolde, where the libretto is limited and there are parts of the opera where a series of musical grunts from the singers might have sufficed. As regards the Ring, Wagner discovered Schopenhauer whilst writing the music to The Valkyrie and, it is suggested that, from then on, it is often the music rather than the libretto which tells us his meaning. (This is not to suggest that the music in the Rhinegold is in any way inferior or less original, far from it. The opening bars of Rhinegold were unlike anything ever heard before). Wagner considered changing Brünnhilde's speech and both Feuerbach-inspired and Schopenhauer-inspired alternative Götterdämmerung libretti were written. I have utilised these in this book. Sensibly Wagner abandoned both of these and kept to the original (see note [32]). In doing so, he argued that he had always been a Schopenhauerian artist but had been unable to recognise this until he had discovered the man's works. He may have been right.

NOTES

Chapter 1

[1] Alberich. Wagner makes no mention of political views for Alberich. Alberich is first seen at the bottom of the Rhine from where he calls the rhinemaidens down to him. The opening is a clear metaphor for the birth of consciousness for which the opening bars have prepared us.

Donnington- Alberich represents the unalloyed grasping self and the rhinemaidens, unattainable longings.

Myth- Alberich is Andvari a semi-aquatic creature. (see note [10])

The political views discussed were held by Wagner for much of the first half of his life (see appendix 'Philosophy')

[2] Rhinemaidens. Not a feature of the Norse Sagas but frequent in medieval lore. Also known as the Lorelei - Rhine mermaids of Koblenz, who, like the Greek Sirens, would lure sailors onto the rocks with their songs. They are variously described as mermaids, water fairies or water nymphs; all are daughters of Father Rhine.
Strangely there is no mention of mermaids in Larousse. There were Egyptian and Phoenician mer-figures. The early Christian church condemned mermaids as symbols of sin: thus ensuring their greatly increased popularity in the first few centuries AD.

Donnington - As mermaids they represent illusions and fantasies, which can be ultimately treacherous if taken too far.

Chapter 2
[3] Wotan's (Odin) eye.
Myth- Wotan gave up his eye in return for a drink from the spring of wisdom, belonging to the wise giant Mimir. This spring arose amongst the roots of the world ash tree (note[30]). The lost eye was subsequently directed inwards in order to gain self-knowledge. Wotan also hung himself from the world ash tree for 9 days with a spear thrust into his own side, after which, he was able to understand the magical runes carved at the base of the tree, thus adding to his store of wisdom. Wotan was just one God of many until around the first century A.D. when his followers claimed him as chief sky God. A large cult following resulted, which lasted for 10 centuries. He had an eight-legged horse, Sleipnir. A typical sacrifice to Wotan would involve hanging from a tree and piercing with a spear. At least some sacrifices seem to have been voluntary although most victims were probably intoxicated. There is an account from a 10th century Arab diplomat, on his way to Russia, of the voluntary sacrifice of a female slave on the burning funeral ship of her master.

Egyptian myth- The Eye of Horus, which Horus lost in battle, symbolises protection and the bringing of wisdom

[4] Fricka. Wagner's representation of convention, law and order, and Wotan's rational aspect, which he would usually prefer to ignore.

Myth - Wotan's wife was Frigg (also Fieja) referred to as queen of the heavens. She shared Wotan's wisdom and was Goddess of marriage, although not entirely faithful herself. Some stories have her as the first Valkyrie.

[5] Valhalla. Wotan's court, described in Prose Edda as containing a wolf and an eagle and being roofed with spears and shields. Sometimes associated with the grave and, as such, a rather gloomy place. Was situated within the massive region of the Gods -Asgard, of early myth. Asgard (not mentioned by Wagner) had a surrounding wall, built by a giant who was cheated out of his full payment by Loki and was subsequently killed by Thor.

[6] Freya. The Goddess Freyja (of the Vanir) was an important but promiscuous Goddess. She was coveted by giants, along with many others.
The Goddess of youth who guarded the golden apples was Idun (also named Holda). She was kidnapped by an eagle, not by giants.

[7] Donner. (German) or Thor (Scand.). The thunder God. A very important figure in myth with a huge cult of his own. Red haired with fearsome powers, his main protagonist was the world serpent.

Froh. The God Freyr, or, maybe, an amalgamation of the Vanir Gods. The Vanir Gods brought peace and plenty rather than austerity and war. Not associated with rainbows particularly. It was actually Freyr, not Donner, who had an incestuous relationship with his twin sister Freyja. (There is no suggestion of this in Wagner.)

Chapter 3

[8] Loge. Loki, trickster demi-God or demon. Associated with fire and smiths. Great friend and blood brother to Wotan but finally the leader of the forces that defeated the Gods in the Götterdämmerung poem (Elder Edda). Capable of being both helpful and destructive at the same time.

[9] Loge/Mime. This relationship in neither in Myth or Wagner

[10] Ring
Myth- Andvari held a great treasure and had the ability to turn himself into a fish. Kidnapped by Loki, he had to pay a ransom of the gold. He tried to retain a ring from the treasure from which he could make further gold but Loki took that as well. Andvari placed a death curse on the ring. Subsequent victims were Fafnir, a giant who obtained the ring by killing his own father and Sigmund. Loki had stolen the gold in order to pay a ransom, requiring him to fill an otter skin with gold. Odin wanted the ring but it was required to finally fill the skin.
In the much later German medieval poem Nibelungenlied, the treasure belonged to King of the Nibelung with Alberich as its guardian. Siegfried appropriated the treasure and was later killed by Hagan acting in the service of his king – Gunther.

Donnington-
Alberich in Wagner stands for our own shadow. Ignore him at your peril.

Chapter 4
[11] Great hero. This is not found in the libretto. Wotan's thoughts are interpreted by the first introduction of Siegfried's musical theme or leitmotiv.

[12] Rainbow. Myth-A massive rainbow called Bifrost acted as a bridge between Asgard and Middle earth.

Chapter 5
[13] Valkyries. Lived with Wotan in Valhalla and behaved much as described by Wagner. They would sometimes wear a swan's plumage and could be made to obey the will of any man who managed to steal this plumage. In Nibelungenlied Hagan stole the plumage of two Valkyries and forced them to reveal certain military secrets.

[14] Volsungs. Wotan's favourite human family.
Myth- A number of generations are chronicled. The founder Sigi was Wotan's son. Sigmund, a later Volsung, who had an incestuous relationship with his sister Signy, was feasting in his hall when an old man with one eye strolled in and plunged a sword into the central tree. No one except Sigmund could draw it out. Later, when it was time for Sigmund to enter Valhalla, the sword smashed against Wotan's spear during a battle. The fragments were later reforged by Sigmund's son, Sigurd or Siegfried (Germ.), an even greater hero.

The followers of Wotan recognised and accepted that Wotan would eventually remove his protection from them just as, one day, Wotan himself would fall.

There were many stories of spirits or humans who would take on the appearances of an animal, especially at night. The animals included otters and eagles but, more commonly, a wolf or a bear. In the Volsung saga Sigmund and Sigurd behave like wolves at one stage.

[15] Central tree. Not totally fanciful. It was the habit of early Germanic tribes to build houses based on a large trunk.

[16] Their love is represented by a burst of some of Wagner's most emotional music. A foretaste of Tristan and Isolde.

[17] There is no explicit physical relationship between Brünnhilde and Wotan in the opera, though the music suggests reconciled lovers by the time she is asleep. It is often suggested that Brünnhilde assumes different persona at different times in the opera. I prefer to see her as evolving.

Myth- Brünnhilde has her swan plumage stolen by King Agnar and, against Wotan's wishes, is forced to help Agnar in battle. As punishment Wotan pricks her with a thorn, which sends her to sleep (Comparison with sleeping beauty story is perhaps too obvious to mention). He then incarcerates her in a wall of fire, as in the opera. Sigurd, riding his horse Gani, awakens her.

Chapter 7
[18] Your very Self.
Donnington- Brünnhilde as anima. Or, in the simpler modern parlance- one's feminine side. Siegfried has previously refused to recognise fear. In this scene he cannot accept a gentler, more philosophical aspect of himself. No wonder he gets into trouble.

Wagner generally prefers to use his music to put his audience through the emotional mangle. Usually he keeps the libretto sparse. Here he utilised his literacy skills to great effect. The libretto in this scene constitutes a moving love poem.

Chapter 8
[19] Mime.
Myth - Regin. Son of Hreidmar to whom Loki had to pay the ransom of the gold in an otter's skin. Regin's brother was Fafnir. The brothers killed their father to obtain the gold but Fafnir took it all and turned into a dragon. Regin became smith to Sigurd, helped him to reforge Sigmund's sword and told Sigurd how to kill Fafnir.
This is a common story, illustrations have been found in: Norway, Sweden, Lancashire and the Isle of Man.

Donnington – Mime is the personification of Siegfried's fear.

[20] Mime later admits to having stolen the sword.

Chapter 9
[21] Dragons.
Myth- (Egyptian) Horus, the Son of Osiris descended to earth as a fire-breathing falcon-winged serpent. The first pictorial representations of obviously dragon-like creatures come from Babylonian civilisations.
Norse myth -long and powerful serpents were sometimes associated with healing as typically occurs further east. The flying, fire-breathing dragon was more common in Anglo- Saxon stories (Beowulf). There are stories in Norse myth adopting such dragons and Fafnir is one example.

[22] Erda. The Myth of the earth mother who: is mother of all things, is associated with the placenta, makes the ground fertile and welcomes us back to the tomb, is pretty well universal and goes back at least to the

Egyptian Goddess Isis. There are Scandinavian tombs dedicated to the earth Goddess from Megalithic times. In some stories, may be Urd, chief of the Norns.

Donnington- (and Wagner?) Erda represents: eternal feminine, earth's anima, basic instinctive knowledge, or maybe just 'common sense'.

[23] Norns.
Myth- Three elderly spinsters: Urd, Verdandi and Skuld, who tend the world ash tree and spin the thread of fate which they hang from the tree. Wotan visited them regularly to learn their findings. Some thought that they held fate and destiny in their hands but, like many elderly spinsters who spend their time spinning, they probably had an over inflated view of their own importance.

Chapter 10
[24] Music. The forest murmurs. Deep longing. A fine example of Wagner's ability to tell us so much more with his music than is obvious in the libretto.

[25] Myth. - a fairly faithful following of the events after Sigurd kills Fafnir (see note[10])

[26] Myth- Grani was Siegfried's horse upon which he rode through the fire. Grani was an offspring of Sleipnir, which itself was the result of a liaison between the horse belonging to the giant who built the wall around Asgard and Loki. Loki took on the form of a mare for the occasion.

[27] There is no such cynicism in the opera. Brünnhilde is firmly and rapturously in love with Siegfried. The music tells us so.

Chapter 11

[28] Wagner has Gunther as the first-born.
In The Volsung saga Sigurd marries Gudrune, the daughter of the King of the Nibelungs. The draught of forgetfulness is given to Sigurd by Gudrun's mother, Grimhilde (the name used by Wagner for Hagan's mother). Siegfried is subsequently killed by the Nibelung family.

The Nibelungenlied, a twelfth Century chivalrous tale of derring-do, has Siegfried as a mediaeval knight and a Prince of the Netherlands, who come to Worms to woo Chriemhilda, sister of King Gunther and niece of Von Troneg Hagan. Gunther desires Brünnhilde who requires to be beaten in trials of strength before she will marry and Siegfried, disguised as Gunther, obliges using a magic cloak, Tarnskappe. In return he is allowed to marry Chriemhilda. Hagan and Gunther subsequently kill Siegfried during a hunt.
Both Gudrune and Chriemhilda take terrible revenge.

[29] Ludwig of Bavaria was Wagner's sponsor, putting up the money for his theatre and championing his cause. We have much to thank him for. He did not have the philistine attitude attributed to the Gibichungs in my text.

[30] The World Ash Tree or Yggdrasil straddled all parts of the earth. It had three roots, one in the underworld or Nifhel where there was a fountain feeding the rivers of earth. The second root was in the land of the giants with a spring watched over by the wise giant Mimir. The third root was related to a well, watched over by the three Norns who watered the tree from the well and protected it against its many dangers: including a serpent coiled around the third root and four stags who

lived in the tree gnawing the young buds. There was also a troublesome squirrel named Ratatosk.

Wagner. -The Norns give us a potted history of Wotan's activities, which does not accord with myth. After giving up his eye, Wotan broke off a branch of the tree to make his spear. The wound on the tree never healed and slowly festered. Eventually the tree started to wither away and the spring feeding the well dried up. After Siegfried shattered his spear, Wotan ordered that the remains of the tree be piled up around Valhalla. He has imprisoned Loge around Brünnhilde's rock for trying to gnaw through the spear. The Norns no longer have the ash tree from which to hang their rope and have to use an unsatisfactory fir tree. After they tell us this story, the rope breaks and they rush off back to Erda, their work of spinning fate is done.

Myth- The ash tree is just about the only item of the old order to survive the Götterdämmerung.

Donnington - His explanation of Wagner's new mythology has considerable merit: the spear standing for human culture and the ash tree and springs for the more natural world. As he puts it " Whole civilisations have declined because their culture has grown too top-heavy to keep in touch with nature and individuals are subject to the same decline. But nature has a way of flooding back as the Rhine floods the last scene of 'Götterdämmerung.'

[31] Saga - Sigurd carries out this act for King Gunnar/Gunther.

[32] In trying to convey the message of the music, rather than the libretto, I've taken great liberties with

Brünnhilde's speech and have utilised the Schopenhauer and Feuerbach inspired libretti. (see appendix 'Philosophy')
Wagner apparently had great trouble deciding on Brünnhilde's speech. Sensibly he decided to leave it close to the original and let the music provide the focus.

What she actually sings may be translated as:
"Like sunlight his clear radiance shines on me:
he was the purest, he who betrayed me!
Deceiving his wife, loyal to his friend,
with his sword he separated himself from his own true love,

No man more honest ever took an oath;
none more true made treaty;
none was more pure in love;
and yet none so betrayed
all oaths, all treaties, his truest love!
Do you know why this was?

(looking upwards)
O you, heavenly custodian of oaths!
Turn your gaze on my great grief,
see your everlasting guilt!
Hear my lament, mighty god!
Through his most doughty deed, that you rightly desired,
you sacrificed him, who wrought it.
For the curse which had fallen on you:
this innocent had to betray me
so that I should become a woman of wisdom!
Do I know now what is your will?
Everything, everything, everything I know,
all is now clear to me!

I hear your ravens stirring with dreaded desired
tidings
I now send them both home.
Rest, rest now, oh God!

Now I take up my inheritance.
Accursed ring, terrible ring,
I take your gold and now I give it away.
Wise sisters of the water's depths,
you swimming daughters of the Rhine,
I thank you for your good counsel.
I give you what you crave:
from my ashes take it for your own!
The fire that consumes me
shall cleanse the ring from the curse!
You in the water, wash it away
and keep pure the gleaming gold
that was disastrously stolen from you.

Fly home, you ravens!
Recount to your master what you have heard here
by the Rhine!
Pass by Brünnhilde's rock: direct Loge, who still
blazes there, to Valhalla;
for the end of the gods is nigh.
Thus do I throw this torch at Valhalla's vaulting
towers.

Grane, my steed, greetings!
Do you too know, my friend, where I am leading
you?
Radiant in the fire, there lies your lord,
Siegfried, my blessed hero.
Are you neighing for joy to follow your friend?
Do the laughing flames lure you to him?
Feel my bosom too, how it burns;
a bright fire fastens on my heart

to embrace him, enfolded in his arms,
to be one with him in the intensity of love!
Heiajoho! Grane! Greet your master!
Siegfried! Siegfried! See! Your wife joyfully greets you!"

[33] Myth- The Götterdämmerung. The Gods had finally brought ruin upon themselves. Tricks like cheating the giant who built the walls of Asgard and numerous thefts and murders have caused a revolt against them. There is great cold. The hordes of wolves, men, serpents and giants led by Loki, bridge the rainbow and there is a massive battle, described in some detail. All are pronounced dead, fire consumes the earth and finally the land sinks beneath the waves. Only Yggdrasil remains, containing the seeds of new men and a new order of Gods. Götterdämmuerung poems and sagas are written in the past tense but presumably were expected to occur in the future. Thus Wagner's title of 'the Ring' is an inspired one and a repeated cycle of events is consistent with myth.

Epilogue
[34] The Rhine originally found the sea in what is now the Bristol Channel in Southern England. In a short cataclysmic event the sea broke through the low lying swamps between mainland Europe and what is now the island of Britain. This occurred only six to seven thousand years ago and there would probably have been associated flooding of the Rhine.

[35] Monotheistic God. This extra pressure on Wotan is not a feature of Wagner. Wagner's Götterdämmerung is the real thing.

[36] Holy fool. Wagnerites (perfect or otherwise) will have no difficulty in recognising this as a reference to 'Parsifal' in which this subject is fully explored.

Bibliography

Robert Donnington   'Wagner's Ring and its Symbols'
Faber & Faber

Bryan Magee   'Wagner and Philosophy'
Penguin

Bernard Shaw   'The Perfect Wagnerite'
Dover Publications

Earnest Newman   'Wagner Nights'
Picador

Ellis H R   'Viking & Norse Mythology'
Chancellor Press

Larousse   'Encyclopaedia of Mythology'
London

Taylor & Auden   'The Elder Edda'
New York,
Random House

Magnusson & Morris   'Volsung Saga The'
Walter Scott Press

Foster- Barnham   'Nibelungenlied The'
Macmillan

Smith G Elliot   'The Evolution of the Dragon'
Kessinger Publications

LINKS

Volsung Saga (full text)
http://www.sacred-texts.com/neu/vlsng/
Nibelungenlied (full text)
http://www.sacred-texts.com/neu/nblng/index.htm
Prose Edda (full text)
http://www.sacred-texts.com/neu/pre/index.htm
The Danish History of Saxo Grammaticus (full text)
http://www.sacred-texts.com/neu/saxo/index.htm
Poetic Edda (full text)
http://www.sacred-texts.com/neu/poe/index.htm

Re Wagner
http://www.trell.org/wagner/motifs.html
http://www.rwagner.net/e-home.html

Re this book
http://alberich4.tripod.com

ISBN 1412026284